SORROW BRINGER

THE FIRE HEART CHRONICLES BOOK 3

JULIANA HAYGERT

COPYRIGHT

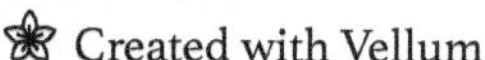 Created with Vellum

AUTHOR'S NOTE

I hope you enjoy reading *Sorrow Bringer*!

Don't forget to sign up for my Newsletter to find out about new releases, cover reveals, giveaways, and more!

If you want to see exclusive teasers, help me decide on covers, read excerpts, talk about books, etc, join my reader group on Facebook: Juliana's Club!

DICTIONARY

Chey – daughter
Chini – son
Daj – mother
Dat – father
Gadjo – non-Romani person
Nais tuke – thank you
Ozi – fire
Phal – brother
Phen – sister
Puri Chey – granddaughter
Puri Chini – grandson
Puri Daj – grandmother
Puri Dat – grandfather
Rom Baro – leader of the enclave
Ruv – wolf/werewolf
Saint Sara-la-Kali – Romani Saint
Sastimos – a greeting
Vurdon – wagon

Yog – fire
Yog Ozi Nas – fire heart fever

1

ANOTHER SLEEPLESS NIGHT.

How many were there now? Ten? Fifteen? I had lost count.

At first, I tried staying in bed and keeping my eyes closed, but my mind wouldn't settle. It raced through so many thoughts, bringing on too many feelings, and I couldn't stay still.

So, even though it was November and cold in Connecticut, I put a heavy coat over my flannel pajamas, and went for a walk around the enclave. At this time of night, everything was quiet. There were only dim lamps located every few feet, illuminating the terracotta houses, the occasional chilly breeze rushing through the narrow streets, and the crunching of the warriors' boots on the stone pavement as they marched along their patrol route.

And the heavy footsteps of the two warriors now following me—Tomas and Leander.

I was already watched and guarded during the day, but it was worse at night.

Ever since we came back from the mountains with the heart flower, cured the sick tziganes, and told the elder council that Damara was still alive and intent on stealing my powers, the security around the enclave had increased tenfold.

And I was forbidden to go to the Bellville enclave.

Since I still wanted to practice magic with Sheila and fighting with Theron, there was only one solution possible: The Bellville enclave would have to move to Lovell.

It hadn't been an easy decision. In fact, it had generated a lot of heated arguments that almost ended in fist fights, but in the end, Neil, the rom baro of the Bellville enclave, agreed that it was the best solution. There were many advantages to this: Lovell had a better structure to protect us, we were stronger in numbers, and I didn't have to go back and forth between enclaves for training, reducing the chances of me being attacked while out.

Out.

We had returned from the mountains three weeks ago, and I still hadn't set one foot out of the enclave.

I was starting to think I never would.

I knew I would, eventually. When another heart flower bloomed and I heard its call, we would have to retrieve it.

Meanwhile, the feeling that never left my chest only increased—I wasn't a queen, despite how they treated me, but a prisoner they lied to.

Sighing, I halted at the edge of the forest and closed my eyes. I pushed those toxic thoughts out of my mind and focused on the sounds of the forest. The sleeping animals, the hooting owls, the dance of the leafless branches in the wind, the rushing waterfall ...

It was okay. Even though the word prisoner popped in my

mind every now and then, I knew it wasn't really the case anymore. I hated being locked inside the enclave, but now, I understood what it meant to be the heart maiden. My life meant nothing if I couldn't help my enclave, my people.

My sole purpose in life was to make sure they were okay. All of them.

I might have resisted that at first, but now when I thought about it, I actually believed it was a noble thing. Something to be proud of.

However, the non-dating rule ...

I let out a deep breath.

I should be okay about that too. It didn't matter if I was the heart maiden and the heart maiden wasn't supposed to be touched. The only guy I wanted to touch wasn't available, and by tzigane laws, he would never be.

I kicked a small rock, then turned and started back through the narrow streets. The two warriors stepped back, rigid like statues, and let me pass. A moment later, they fell into step behind me.

If I didn't know them outside their posts as warriors, I would think they never cracked a smile. Well, I didn't know Leander that well, but I had spent some time with Tomas, since he was Ryane's fiancée, and he had always smiled and laughed and been super sweet whenever he wasn't on duty.

A dull sting began in the back of my mind, and a plethora of images exploded in my head. Damara holding the heart flower. Felix walking into the cave. Artan leaning over me beside the lake. Cianna telling me she was my grandmother. Damara appearing in the cave tunnels. Cianna dying in my arms. My arms bathed in blood. My body consumed by fire.

"Mirella, are you okay?"

I shook my head. The pain and the images disappeared.

I glanced over my shoulder and found Tomas and Leander right behind me, watching over me. I forced a small smile. "Just a little tired," I said. It wasn't entirely a lie. I was plagued by insomnia. I was tired. Exhausted. "I'm fine."

Trying to pretend nothing had happened, I resumed walking, and they waited a few steps before following me again. But something had happened. That pain and those images, they had assaulted me before. It had started a couple of days after we returned from the mountains, but thankfully, it hadn't happened often, only once every three or four days.

Talking to my friends and my mother about it crossed my mind, but I always ended up pushing that idea away. The pain, the images, and the insomnia were stress from knowing Damara was still alive and after me. Once we dealt with her, or I got used to the fact that there was a powerful, evil tzigane out for my blood, I was sure it would go away.

My thoughts were so out of it, I hadn't even noticed where my feet were taking me until I halted in front of the fountain in the center of the main square.

I glanced down the dark water—soon, the water would be emptied before it froze—at the dark silhouette staring back at me.

Sometimes I didn't recognize myself.

"You should be sleeping."

I sucked in a sharp breath and straightened. "Can't sleep."

I sensed as he stopped a couple of steps away, his tall, powerful body angled toward mine. "This isn't the first time. Everything okay?"

How dare he ask me that? He knew everything was not okay.

Bracing myself, I turned and stared him.

Holy shit, Artan was so handsome; there was no way to

brace myself. He wore the usual warrior's uniform—brown suede pants and vest, a beige thermal tunic underneath, combat boots, plus a thick leather jacket—and yet he managed to look more composed, more lethal than the other warriors.

Frowning, I glanced around. Tomas and Leander were gone. Artan had probably sent them away.

Crap, I would rather he left me alone.

I crossed my arms. "What do you want, Artan?"

He ran a hand through his light brown. "You have been avoiding me."

"True."

"Mirella ... I know you're hurt, but we should talk about—"

"There's nothing to talk about," I snapped. "You're engaged. Period."

That had been a surprise, and I hadn't been prepared for it. In some ways, it felt even worse than finding out Damara was alive. Because Damara was crazy and evil. We expected bad things from evil beings.

But Artan? Artan had been my rock, my foundation. The man lived and breathed honor. Then, he kissed me, and a week later, I found out he was promised to someone else.

And he had never bothered to mention that.

Artan pressed his lips into a thin line. "There's much more to it than that."

"It doesn't matter, does it? Nothing has changed."

"You do know you're not supposed to be touched, right?"

I gaped at him. "So that makes it all right? You kissed me, then regretted it, but oh wait, it's okay, because you're not going to be with me anyway."

His nostrils flared. "That's not what I meant."

"Don't you get it? It doesn't matter what you meant or what your intention was. You deceived me, and you'll marry Kizzy."

I had tried redirecting my anger toward the young woman, but I couldn't. Much like I had done with Artan, I had avoided her, but the enclave was small, and I still bumped into her every so often. And she was always smiling and saying the nicest things, and helping out with the elders and the children. She was pretty, too. Beside her, I felt like I was riddled with faults. How could I compete with an angel?

Then again, there was no competing.

Tzigane marriage agreements were rarely broken, and why would they break it? It wasn't like Artan could be with me instead. The elder council would never allow it.

So, why couldn't he be with her and be happy?

I just didn't think I could spend the rest of my life standing here, watching as Artan married Kizzy, then had mini-Artans and mini-Kizzies with her.

The thought hurt too much.

Anger and hurt and jealousy molded around my heart.

Artan let out a long breath. "Okay. Be mad at me all you want. Blame it all on me. Don't talk to me if you don't want to. But we have to practice your fighting skills, Mirella. It's important."

"I am training with Theron."

He shook his head. "We've talked about this before. You know it's important for you to train with different people so you learn different fighting styles." He paused. "You can punch me all you want during training."

Was he trying to joke right now? Was he serious? I gritted my teeth. "That makes sense, but I would rather have Ramon teach me."

He knew Ramon, Theron's brother, didn't like me much. Which probably would make him a good adversary, since he wouldn't go easy on me, but perhaps not the best teacher.

"Mirella, please."

"That's enough, Artan." I couldn't take it anymore. Artan begging? I couldn't stomach it. He was a strong warrior, and I wanted that image of him in my mind.

Without another word, I spun on my heels and started back to my house.

He followed me. "Mirella, wait."

"I would like to be alone."

"You know I can't do that. I dismissed the other warriors so I have to stay with you."

Frustration whipped through me. I clenched my hands, trying to control my feelings before I jumped at him and squeezed his throat. Couldn't he be at least more considerate? He had hurt me. He knew that. Then why couldn't he give me space?

"Just ... stay as far as you can, then." I walked a little faster.

I heard him whisper, "Mirella," but thankfully he didn't argue. He followed me through the streets in silence, a shadow that made me uncomfortable.

I turned the last corner onto my street and slowed down as I walked past the big house where most of the Bellville tziganes now lived. It was a three-story house with a warm terracotta color and several tall windows and wooden flower boxes. The married couples had been given their own houses, but Neil, Dolan, Sheila, Theron, Ramon, Cora, Rye, Nico, Shay, Marie, and Anne shared this big manor.

Something tugged in my mind and an image of a building on fire filled my mind.

A horrid scream pushed that image aside, and I stared at the house. It was coming from inside.

The scream came again, and I ran up the four steps leading to the front door. I turned the knob, but the door was locked.

"I can do it," Artan said, stepping to my side. He placed his hand in front of the keyhole and sent his air magic into the lock. It clicked and turned. He pushed the door open for me. "Here you go."

I raced to the stairs and found Rye and Theron in the hallway, looking confused.

"Mirella, what are you doing here?" Ramon asked from his suite's door.

"I heard someone screaming," I said.

The scream echoed through the second floor hallway, louder in here than it was outside.

"It's Cora," Rye said, his eyes wide.

We all rushed to her suite at the end of the hallway. Rye burst in and we followed. I halted in my tracks as I took in the scene: Cora in her bed, twisting and grunting as if she had been possessed.

2

───────

IN A MATTER OF SECONDS, CORA'S ROOM WAS FILLED WITH most of the manor's residents. We crowded around her bed, trying to wake her up from whatever terror she was fighting.

"Cora," Nico called out. "Wake up."

Rye rested a hand on her forehead. "Please, Cora, wake up."

Covered in sweat, Cora's back arched up and she screamed again.

"She's having a nightmare," Sheila said from the end of the bed. She had her eyes closed and her hands on her temples. She was inside Cora's mind. "I'm trying to pull her from it, but I can't." She grunted and struggled a little longer. Then, she opened her eyes and dropped her hands. "She kicked me out."

Cora screamed again, a hair-raising sound that tugged at my heart.

I didn't really know what I was doing, but I had to try something. "Hold her down," I told Rye.

He placed his big hands on her shoulders, while she

jerked from side to side, and stabilized her a little. Channeling my magic, I laid my hands on her forehead and her chest, right above her breasts. I had better control over my magic now, but I was still afraid I would get carried away and burn her without meaning to. Carefully, I sent some of the warmth from my fire into her, to bring her comfort. The process was slow, but Cora relaxed. Her jerky movements reduced, her breathing slowed down, and her screams stopped.

When she seemed to be just sleeping, I pulled my hands away.

"Cora?" Rye asked. Anguish laced his voice. Everyone knew he loved her, and even though she denied it, Cora loved him too. It was heartbreaking to watch Rye wait for her to wake. "Cora, please, wake up."

A sob ripped out of her mouth. Tears streamed down from her closed eyes. Cora sat up and hugged her knees, hiding her face from view.

"Cora, are you okay?" Nico asked in a low voice.

Rye ran a hand down her back. "Want to talk about it?"

She shook her head.

"I think the nightmare was about her enclave," Sheila whispered. "There were alchemists and heart animals and fire. A lot of fire."

Cora lifted her head and wiped at her cheeks. "It wasn't a nightmare. It was a memory." Rye's hand stilled.

Nico sighed. "Oh, Cora."

A little over three years ago, Cora, Rye, and Nico had moved to Bellville after their enclave had been attacked by alchemists and burned to the ground. The three of them were the sole survivors of the massacre.

"I'll go make some chamomile tea," Sheila said before

leaving the room. Neil, Dolan, Ramon, Shay, and even Artan mumbled something about helping and followed her out.

"I'm sorry," Cora said, her voice breaking with another sob. "I haven't dreamed about it in such a long time. I thought I was finally over it."

"It's okay." Rye wrapped his arms around her. "It's okay. It'll always hurt. We'll never forget any of it."

Nico sniffed as tears filled his eyes, and Theron retreated to the window. He stared out as if there was something interesting calling to him from the streets below.

Theron hadn't seen the destruction happen, but he had seen the aftermath. He had been the one to go back and check for survivors—and confirm there were none. After that, he helped Cora, Rye, and Nico fight the alchemists and come to Bellville.

It was a sad story. My stomach curled just imagining the horror of it all.

"You know you can always talk to us about it, right?" I rubbed her shoulder.

She pulled back from Rye's embrace and wiped her tears once more. "There's not much to talk about. Things are distorted and worse in my dreams, but the pain is the same." She let out a long, calming breath. "I'm okay. I'm better. But I don't think I can go back to sleep now."

"It's okay." Nico pulled out one of the two chairs from the corner of her suite to her bedside and sat down. "We can just talk the rest of the night."

I knew I wasn't going to sleep anyway, so I grabbed the other chair and sat down beside Nico. "Me too."

"Scoot over," Rye said, settling down beside her in bed. Even though it was a queen and had plenty of space for both of them, Cora only moved a few inches, and Rye had to sit with his side pressed to hers.

The love shining from his eyes as he looked at her! Jealousy festered inside me. Oh, how I wanted someone to look at me that way, to love me for me.

Cora smiled through the tears. "*Nais tuke*, guys."

Theron cleared his throat. "I'll tell Sheila we'll need more tea. And maybe something to eat too."

"Good one," Nico said. Then Theron was gone and Nico turned to me. He whispered, "I heard you landed a nice punch on his chin the other day."

Rye nodded. "I heard that, too."

Me punch Theron? Had they seen him? There was no way I could land a punch on him. Theron was a tall warrior with strong arms and wide shoulders. His dark hair down to his shoulder and piercing dark eyes added to his mysterious persona, but deep down, he was a big teddy bear. He was intense and strong and passionate. He was also crushing on my best friend, and I totally supported it.

"I wish. Well, my fist grazed his chin, but it wasn't on purpose." I snorted. "I tripped and fell."

"Ah, no." Nico frowned. "And I almost bet that you had punched him for real."

My eyes widened. "Wait. There's a bet?"

Nico paled. "Well ..."

A small laugh came from Cora. "Some guys, mainly the warriors, are betting when or if you're gonna be as good as Theron in fighting. But it's all just for fun."

I frowned, then I smiled. "Can I bet too? Because I bet I'll never be anywhere close to as good as Theron. Or any of you."

Rye laughed and Cora smiled. She tilted her head. "You

know, I can spar with you some time. I bet it would be fun. And, like Theron always says, the more people you fight, the better warrior you will become."

I perked up. Sparring with Cora would be a hundred times better than sparring with Artan. "Would you do that?"

"Sure," she said.

"I can do it too," Rye said.

"That's great."

"Hm, don't even look at me," Nico said before I had done anything. "I'm not a warrior."

"It's okay," I said, feeling lighter than I had in days. I guess spending some time with friends was good enough to lift my spirits. I made a mental note to do something with them all. Since I couldn't go out to the nightclub anymore, and they hadn't gone because I couldn't, I could invite them all to my house one night and we could have a party there. I liked that idea.

Minutes later, Theron and Sheila brought the tea and cookies and we talked for hours.

My schedule was pretty tight, but I needed a break from being the heart maiden, when I was just Mirella.

I JERKED AWAKE, CONFUSED ABOUT WHERE I WAS AND WHAT WAS happening. Sitting up, I realized I was lying in Cora's bed, a throw blanket over my legs. Bright light filtered through the dark curtains. I grabbed my cell phone from the pillow beside me and checked the time. It was almost noon!

What the hell happened?

I pushed up from the bed, stopped by the bathroom, washed my face, ran my fingers through my messy curls, then exited the suite. The corridor was eerily quiet as I walked past the several closed doors—was everyone sleeping?—and went downstairs. I heard a soft noise coming from the back of the house.

Sheila and Dolan were in the kitchen, cooking.

"Hand me that, please?" Sheila said, pointing to a pot over the island.

"Yes, *daj*," Dolan said, turning to get the bowl. He saw me approaching, and his eyes widened for a moment. "Good morning, Mirella."

Heat of embarrassment spread through my cheeks. "Morning."

Sheila spied me over her shoulder. "Sit down and I'll make you something to eat."

"Hm." I brushed my hands on my jeans. "I don't think I have time for that. Darcy is probably already on a manhunt for me."

Sheila smiled. "You're fine. Don't worry."

"What do you mean?"

"Theron told Darcy earlier that you were taking the morning off," Dolan said. "He also warned Risa, in case she saw your bedroom empty and became worried." Wow, they had thought of everything. Dolan pulled up a stool from the island and gestured to it. "Now sit and eat."

Still a little wary that Darcy would just have agreed to that, I sat down at the chair. "I'm confused, though. What happened?"

Sheila dropped the pot she was messing with and grabbed a plate from the cupboard. "Theron told me that you fell asleep in a chair. So, he put you in Cora's bed, and they all left the room to let you sleep." She grabbed a couple of muffins from a wicker basket and put them on the plate. "He said you haven't been sleeping much." She brought the plate to me.

Dolan placed a mug with tea and a glass with orange juice beside the plate. "Let me know if you want something else."

I reached for the tea. "Thanks."

Ramon entered the kitchen. He skidded to a stop when he saw me. His eyes wide, he shifted his gaze to his father, who met his stare, then lowered his head. Frowning, Ramon approached the island.

"Feeling better?" he asked, taking a muffin from the wicker basket.

"Hm, yes." What the hell was that exchange between father and son? And why was Ramon asking how I was feeling? He didn't care about anyone other than his father and brother.

He dipped his chin. "Good." After another heated glanced at his father, Ramon walked out of the kitchen.

What was that about?

"Tell me about not sleeping *at all*," Sheila prompted as she brought more food to the island: fruit, toast, cheese spread, honey, and syrup.

During our magic practice, we talked a lot and I had already told her about not sleeping well, but I didn't tell her how bad it really was so I wouldn't worry her.

But, if there was one person I could talk to about this, then Sheila was the best person. "I just ... can't sleep. I lie in bed and my mind races, nonstop. My body feels restless, like I need to walk, or run, or dance." I could go on. I could tell her about it all. About the images that flashed in my mind at unexpected times and the dull ache in the back of my skull. But for some reason, I didn't want to tell her about that. Perhaps because mentioning it made it real? Perhaps it was because I liked when she looked at me with a worried glint in her eyes, and I didn't want to risk having that changed into wariness. Suspicion. Fear. I shrugged. "I don't know why."

Sheila glanced at Dolan, then back at me. What? Did they know something I didn't? She leaned over the island. "Have you been stressed out about being the heart maiden?"

I almost laughed at that. "I thought that had been established months ago!"

"Yes, I remember how you resisted becoming the heart maiden, but I thought that had changed."

"It changed. I've fully accepted it now."

She narrowed her eyes at me. "Have you?"

I stared at her, not sure what she meant by that. "Yes. I have."

With a heavy sigh, Sheila pushed away from the table. "All right. I'll add some meditation time during our practices to try to calm your mind. Hopefully, that will help you sleep better."

That actually sounded like a good plan. "Thank you."

"Now eat up!" She pointed to the food on the island before turning her back to me and going back to whatever she was cooking before I came into the kitchen.

Even though I had barely touched my tea, Dolan refilled my mug. Then he mumbled something about having to talk to Neil and left. If I had to bet, I would say Neil was with the elder council at the moment. As the rom baro of Bellville, he had been invited to assist the elder council, something which probably irritated Darcy to no end. Sheila and Dolan had been invited too, but both of them said they wanted no part in whatever the elder council did. Although it didn't seem like he was excited about it, Neil participated because Bellville should be represented somehow.

I hadn't even finished eating when Sheila mentioned serving lunch soon. She invited me to stay and eat with the others, but I had to get going. I had already skipped my responsibilities for the morning. I shouldn't bail on the entire day.

After helping clean up and thanking Sheila for the brunch and her care, I left. As expected, the moment my feet touched the stone pavement of the street, two warriors fell into formation behind me.

I sighed and adjusted my coat. The sun was high in the sky, but the air was too chilly for my taste.

I took five steps before I halted again.

A young woman with light brown curls strolled toward me. "Mirella! It's so good to see you."

My stomach twisted in knots. "Hi, Kizzy."

Artan's fiancée stopped in front of me, her smile easy and true. "You've been so busy lately, I've barely seen you around the enclave."

I nodded. "Thus the life of a heart maiden."

"I'm so glad we have a new heart maiden," she said. Everything about this girl looked pure and innocent. "And you haven't been sleeping much. I hope that's not messing with your tight schedule."

I frowned. "How do you know that?"

"Oh." She let out a chuckle. "Artan told me. He talks a lot about you."

I swallowed a gasp. He did? Why? By now, Kizzy probably knew he was one of my fighting instructors and the one in charge of my security—he set up who would follow me around and when. But ... there was more? Why would he talk to her about me?

Nervous about this entire situation, I looked down at my

hands. "Don't believe everything he says. When I mess up during training, he gets mad at me and starts spouting lies." That was the only thing, the only *lie*, I could think of saying.

"Oh, no, he adores you." I blinked. What had she said? And what was with that smile and warmth in her eyes. She wasn't kidding. "I mean, the entire enclave adores you. You're our heart maiden after all."

"O-of course," I muttered. Holy crap. This was too awkward. "I need to get going. I have a lot of things to do."

"Sure." She stepped to the side, allowing me to pass.

"Thank you." I glanced at her once more as I walked past her.

I was about to say bye when she said instead, "Oh, and Mirella, please take good care of my man."

I almost tripped on my feet. "W-what?"

She chuckled again. "Training with him, you're bound to become a great warrior. Just don't hurt him too much when you do. I don't like to see him suffering."

My man ...

My heart squeezed. "I'll keep that in mind."

3

I SHOULD HAVE GONE TO THE TRAINING CENTER, OR TO THE elder council room to apologize for missing my morning duties, but after sleeping in someone else's bed, being in the same clothes for twenty-four hours, and bumping into Kizzy on the street, I felt icky. In desperate need of a bath, I went straight home.

"Mom?" I called out once I stepped inside and locked the front door.

"In the kitchen!"

I walked past the foyer, down the hallway, and through the kitchen's archway, and stopped in my tracks.

"Ellie? What are you doing here?"

My best friend stood from the stool she had been sitting on and rushed to me. "I just missed you." She embraced me.

I returned her embrace. "But ..." I frowned. "It's Tuesday. Don't you have classes?" I pulled back and narrowed my eyes at her. "You're not here to see me. You're here to see Theron."

Red tinted her cheeks. It was actually pretty cute with her strawberry blond curls and blue eyes. "Well ..."

I elbowed her. "Don't lie to me."

"Mirella, stop bugging your friend," my mother said. She put two teacups and a steaming teapot on the island. "Now come here and tell me what happened. You have no idea the scare I had when Theron showed up at my door this morning."

I stared at her. My mother wasn't one for talking, especially chatting. And she was asking me what happened as if she really wanted to sit down and talk about it over tea. What was going on?

"You're still not sleeping well?" Ellie asked.

"Didn't I just sleep for what ..." I had to count it in my head. "For over seven hours! That's great in my book."

"Well, yes, but that was after not sleeping for days," my mother said. "You probably collapsed from being too tired."

"It's okay now, though," I assured her. "Sheila said she'll add some exercises to our practice to help me relax. Those should help when I go to bed."

"Good." My mother nodded. "That's good." She turned to the cutting board.

"Mom, I just ate. I'm not having lunch anytime soon."

"Oh. Okay." Her hand slowed down as she cut the carrots in little pieces, but she didn't stop.

I felt bad, but I wouldn't force myself to eat to please her. If she wanted to, she could still cook for Ellie and herself. I would eat whatever she made later for dinner.

I nudged Ellie and the two of us went to the living room at the front of the house. Bringing our tea, we sat down on the couch.

"So ..." I wiggled my eyebrows at her. "Does Theron know you're here?"

Her cheeks reddened some more. "He might."

"Okay, wait. How serious are you two?" I knew they had been flirting since we had come back from the mountains almost three weeks ago, but had they moved past that?

"I don't know," she said. "We've been texting, and when I come here, I end up seeing him, but mostly when he's with you."

"Have you two kissed?" I had to ask.

"No," she whispered. "And that worries me! Doesn't he like me? Why hasn't he kissed me yet?"

I laughed. "Calm down. It's because tziganes are different from *gadjos*."

She frowned. "What do you mean?"

"Well, I don't know much. I wasn't raised in this culture, and I'm not allowed to love someone or be touched." She knew that, of course. "But from what I've seen, they put more emphasis on courtship."

"That's romantic."

"It seems to be." Since I couldn't have that, I would never know.

I sighed.

And I wasn't sure if Ellie and Theron could ever have that either. Being a *gadjo* meant Ellie wasn't allowed inside the enclave, much less to date a tzigane. She was only here right now because I had made it clear I wanted her to be able to visit me freely. Darcy fought me on it, but Artan said he would talk to the warriors guarding the entrance and make sure she got in whenever she came over.

But if the elder council found out she was here? They would throw a fit. And if they found out she was interested in Theron and Theron in her? I honestly didn't know what would happen. Probably a new war would erupt, because

Bellville wouldn't bow down to Lovell's rules, but Lovell would try to impose them nevertheless.

Oh, the mess it would be.

Whatever they decided, though, I would support them. In my opinion, Ellie and Theron were a cute couple.

"What's up next on your busy heart maiden agenda?" Ellie asked in a teasing tone.

I rolled my eyes. "I have practice with Theron, actually, then a meeting with the elder council. And, if I still have time after that, I want to stop by the evening dance class."

"Can't stop being a ballerina?"

I shook my head. "Never. And I don't care if the elder council doesn't like it, I want to participate in the kids' class as much as I can." I smiled. "I miss teaching kids. I'm not a teacher here, but just being among them during class makes me feel better. More like myself."

Ellie reached over and patted my hand. "It's time you figured out that you're not that old Mirella anymore. You're a new Mirella now. You should be your new self now."

I scrunched my nose. "Have you been reading any inspiration books or something lately?"

She laughed.

Her laughter grew and exploded inside my skull. A ringing noise that brought out that pain, that dull pain that thrummed and thrummed until it too grew out of control and drove me to my knees.

"Mirella!"

I heard her call, but once again, her words were distorted and became a scream inside my head. I closed my eyes and pressed my hands to my ears, willing it all to stop.

Instead, images flashed before my eyes.

Half a dozen alchemists dressed in their black clothes and

masks, holding their shadow daggers in their hands, advancing toward me.

Felix roaring and stomping around his cage, trying to bite anyone who got too close.

Damara dancing in the enclave's main square, with the heart flower in her hands. She laughed out loud and burned alive whoever dared get too close.

Artan reaching his hand into my chest and ripping my beating heart out.

Muma Padurii and her wyverns atop the enclave's main building, sending curses down on us.

Cora and Ellie laughing at me while I fought Theron during practice and failed miserably.

The images raced in front of my eyes, making me dizzy.

I curled into a ball, trying to fight against the pain and the nausea and the sounds and images.

"Mirella, listen to me."

I knew this voice. Even if it pierced my mind and brought on more pain, I knew this voice. I wanted to reach for it. But the pain was so strong, so potent, it crippled me. Tremors ran through my body as the images continued.

Alchemists surrounded me inside my house.

Felix breaking through the door.

Damara jumping around my bedroom.

Artan winking at me while holding Kizzy's hand.

Muma Padurii setting the wyvern free in my backyard.

Cora and Ellie knelt beside me, watching me writhe in pain, but doing nothing.

"Open your mouth, *chey*."

I didn't know what was going on. The pain made it impossible to differentiate reality and the hallucinations in my head. I pressed my trembling hands over my eyes.

Then, something bitter dripped down my throat and agonizingly slow my tremors lessened. My breathing slowed. The pain reduced. The visions went away.

When I regained control, I was sprawled on the living room floor, my mother and Ellie bent over me.

"Are you okay now, *chey*?" my mother asked. The tightness of her voice, the worried glint in her gaze—it scared me.

I thought for a minute. "I think so."

Ellie and my mother offered me their hands and pulled me up. I glanced around and gasped. The living room was a mess. The coffee table was turned, two chairs had been pushed back, a picture frame was broken, one decorative pillow was ripped into ribbons, another had a big black mark as if it had been burnt, and the rest were scattered around the floor.

"What happened?" I asked.

"You tell me!" my mother rasped. I could see she was trying to control the tone of her voice. "I've never seen you like that. I thought you were going to hurt Ellie."

The blood rushed from my face. "W-what?"

"I'm okay," Ellie said. "It's okay. But when whatever started, you were thrashing like a mad woman. I think your magic flared." She pointed to the burnt pillow. "I felt like I was trying to hold on to a rabid tiger."

Holy shit. "I'm so sorry." I glanced to my mother. "I don't know what that was. It's never happened before."

She pressed her lips into a thin line. "I don't know either."

"What did you give me?"

"A strong calming elixir. It was the only thing I could think of." She sighed. "I ended up using a large dose. In the next five minutes, you'll feel incredibly sleepy, and in the next ten, you'll be deep asleep."

I gaped at her. "What?"

"Come on." She reached for me. "Let's go to bed before you pass out here, and poor Ellie and I have to drag you to your bedroom."

I took a step back. "I can't … I have too much to do now."

"Mirella, *chey*." My mother sucked in a sharp breath. "You won't be able to do anything right now. You'll sleep. For quite some time, actually. So, just listen to me, okay? Let's go to your bedroom."

I opened my mouth to argue with her, but I felt it. A slow wave of tiredness washing over my body. Inch by inch, it surrounded me, making me tired, sleepy.

"Okay," I whispered.

With Ellie's and my mother's help, I went upstairs to my suite and lay down in bed—without taking a much needed shower and changing my clothes.

"Think of this as making up for all the nights you haven't slept," my mother said. She offered me a small smile. "Now just close your eyes and rest."

"Good night," Ellie said.

I wanted to reply to her, but my mouth felt heavy. My eyelids too.

Before I knew it, I fell into a deep sleep.

4

____

THE FIRST SIGHT I ENCOUNTERED AFTER I OPENED MY EYES almost gave me a heart attack.

"Finally, you're awake," Darcy said, her tone tight. The old hag was seated on an armchair beside my bed, her legs crossed and her hands folded above her knee. Her dark eyes regarded me with arrogance, disgust. I didn't know what her problem was with me, but the feeling was mutual.

Grunting, I sat up and checked the time on my phone. It was already mid-morning. Which meant I had slept for almost fifteen hours. For someone who had barely slept in days, I had gotten my fair share of snoozes the past twenty-four hours. Why did I still feel weak and a little dizzy? It was probably from sleeping too much.

I scooted to the edge of my bed. "What do you want?"

"I'm here as an elder council member. We want to know what's going on. Why are you neglecting your duties?"

A groan took root at the base of my throat, but I pushed it down. Arguing with the old hag would only bring me more trouble.

"I haven't slept well, which makes me tired during the day," I told her the truth. "I think the lack of sleep caught up to me."

She narrowed her eyes at me. "So you slept all day yesterday?"

"It wasn't all day." I gritted my teeth. Why did talking to her put me on edge? At first, I felt bad for not liking her, after all, she was the head of the elder council and Artan's grandmother. But now I just didn't care. "I woke up and had plans to go to training in the afternoon."

"What happened, then?"

I pushed up from the bed, trying to think of something. How could I tell her the truth and lie at the same time? "I felt a little dizzy after sleeping at an odd time and not eating well, so my mother made me a calming tea. I think she overdid it, because I went out."

Darcy pressed her lips into a thin line. Could she see past me? Did she know I was telling her only half the truth? On instinct, I checked the walls around my mind. They were up and strong. I would like to think Darcy would never try such a vile thing, but honestly, I wasn't sure.

Darcy pushed up from the chair. "How are you feeling now?"

Giving her my back, and knowing it was deemed rude, I walked to my closet's door. "I'm going to take a shower, eat something. And ... I don't know. I have to see how I'll feel later." I glanced at the old hag. "Don't worry, Darcy. I know my duties, and I know this is day number two of me *ignoring* them. Believe me, it's not because I want to."

She took three steps toward me then halted, her eyes cold. "Let me know if anything else happens. If you're still weak or tired or can't sleep. The elder council is here to help you, but for that, we need to know *exactly* what happens to you."

"Will do," I answered.

"I'll be going, then." She walked to the door, then paused and looked at me again. "I know your *gadjo* friend is inside the enclave again." What? Ellie was still here? "You know it's forbidden to bring *gadjos* in, even if they know about us. Please, tell her to leave at once."

Oh, I wouldn't budge on this. "She's my friend, and she's welcome here."

Darcy's nostrils flared. "We have rules, Mirella. We have to follow those rules if we want a peaceful, harmonious community. And one of those rules is no *gadjos* in the enclave."

I crossed my arms. "Then you better make an amendment to that rule saying Ellie is welcomed here at any time."

"I don't like your tone."

"That's because you heard it right. It's a threat. Allow Ellie to come and go as she pleases, or we'll have problems. More than we already do. Do you think I'm difficult? Test me, and you'll find out just how difficult I can be."

Her mouth hit the floor. "Excuse me?"

"You heard me."

Darcy grimaced, but didn't lose her composure. "We'll talk more about this later."

"I'm looking forward to it."

After a grunt, Darcy marched out of my bedroom and closed the door behind her.

Old hag.

The elder council was here to help me? I always felt like they wanted to put a chain around my neck and treat me like their little dog. I could only go so far, and if I didn't obey, I wouldn't get a treat.

Then I met Damara and she had warned me the elder council was not what I thought it was. She said they were hiding things, lying to me. I hated to admit, but sometimes I wondered if she was right.

A shudder ran up my spine.

It was hard to think Damara was alive and out there, and only Saint Sarah-la-Kali knew doing what. The way she was so quiet after revealing herself? It scared me.

My bedroom's door opened again, and I stumbled back, my heartbeat spiking.

Ellie spied inside. "Hi."

I put my hand over my racing heart. "Holy crap, you startled me."

She stepped inside. "Sorry. I was just hiding from the old hag."

I smiled at her. "Don't worry. I just threatened to rain on her parade if she continues insisting on sending you out."

She gaped at me. "You did what?"

I chuckled. "It's fine. She needs me. They all do. They won't go against this one wish, I'm sure."

"Still, I don't like the way she looks at me. I feel like a fly she'll squash with her shoe."

I rolled my eyes. "Oh, Ellie. That's quite the visual." I picked up some ripped jeans and a thin sweater from my closet and headed to my bathroom. "Have you gone home at all since yesterday?"

"Nope." She opened up her jacket and showed me the shirt she was wearing: one of my long sleeve thermal tees. "I think it's time I left a change of clothes here."

"Please do so. I'm sure that will make Darcy's fury spike."

Her eyes widened. "Then maybe I shouldn't."

"But I want that to happen."

I winked and disappeared inside the bathroom. After a long, hot shower, I put on my clothes and met Ellie and my mother in the kitchen. It was almost noon again and I was famished. While we talked about school and dance classes and missed practices, Ellie and I set up the breakfast table beside the kitchen. My mother finished making brunch for us.

"Are you really feeling better?" My mother asked for the hundredth time.

I swallowed the big bite of pancakes. "I am. I swear." To be honest, there was still a lingering dull pain in the back of my skull and a little dizziness, but that was nothing compared to before. I could easily ignore those. "That's why I'm going to the training grounds in a little bit."

"No," my mother snapped. "You had something ... big yesterday, something we don't understand. Until we know more, you should rest."

"One, what if we don't find out anything for weeks? I can't stop training for that long. And two, I'm sure it was lack of sleep. I've slept a lot for the past two days. I should be fine now."

"I still think you should take it easy," my mother argued.

"Mi, I think your mother is right," Ellie said, her voice low. "You should take the rest of the day off, at least."

"Don't you two know me?" I stared at them. "I'm a restless person. I can't stay still. After all this sleeping, I'm already sick of being in bed. Inside the house for that matter. If I don't resume my training, then I need to stretch my legs at least."

"Then you should take Ellie with you," my mother suggested.

"W-what?" Ellie croaked.

"Mom, Ellie is a wanted woman right now. I just had an

argument with Darcy because of her."

"By Saint Sara-la-Kali," my mother whispered.

"It's better if Ellie stays out of sight for a little while."

As expected, my mother didn't drop the subject so easily. She argued with me that I shouldn't go out. If I wanted to go, then I could go to the backyard and walk there. With the size of our backyard, it would take me ten steps to walk the perimeter. That wouldn't do.

Besides, I reminded her the warriors would probably follow my every step. If I felt bad, weak, or dizzy, they would know right away.

To confirm I was right, my mother watched from the front door as I stepped out and two warriors stepped out from the shadows and fell into formation behind me. Staring at her, I gestured toward them as if I was saying "told ya!" but she only rolled her eyes at me and disappeared inside the house.

I was a little sad about leaving Ellie stuck inside the house —I knew how that felt—but I needed a few minutes outside.

To my surprise, I didn't encounter too many familiar faces around the streets. It was early afternoon. The kids were probably in school and everyone else had work to do. Even though the enclave didn't function as a normal town, everyone had jobs and duties, which kept them busy most of the day.

On a normal day, I would have been at the training grounds with Theron. I had no idea what he was up to now, since he had just gotten the afternoon off, but I was sure he had found something to keep him busy.

I walked around aimlessly—or at least I thought I had, until I halted in front of the dance studio. Classes and dance groups met early mornings and in the evenings, so right now, it was empty.

Knowing exactly what I had to do to relax and feel more like myself, I went inside the building—anywhere else in the world, a dance studio would be locked when no one was using it. Here in the enclave, most buildings were always open, even in the middle of the night.

The warriors followed me inside, but thankfully, they stayed at the front room when I stepped into the biggest classroom.

Inhaling deeply, I dragged my feet over the floor, taking in the wall covered in mirrors and the barre at the opposite wall. I had been here three days ago while a group of kids had flamenco classes, but entering this place alone? It suddenly felt so right. So me.

I kicked my boots off, slipped my jacket from my arms, took my phone out of my pocket, and pressed play on one of my favorite flamenco songs. I put the jacket and my phone down, and closed my eyes.

I let the melody of the song wash over me, the beat of the rhythm fill my veins, carry me. I didn't think as I moved. I just did it, as if dancing had always been a part of me, as if I had been born knowing how to dance, as if there was nothing else in the world I should do other than dance. Not even being a heart maiden. Not even saving an entire race from extinction.

Dancing was my calling, I was sure of it.

The beat pushed me. My curls whipped side to side while I stomped my feet, rolled my hips, waved my arms, and turned into fast pirouettes.

I was lost in the moment; I barely sensed it. A new energy brushed against my mind, making itself known. Confused, I stopped and opened my eyes.

Someone was watching me from the door.

5

"DON'T STOP," ARTAN SAID.

I gaped at him. "What the hell? What are you doing here?"

He cleared his throat. "I heard you were out and wanted to make sure you were okay." He jerked his chin toward me. "I guess you are."

I crouched down and grabbed my phone and jacket. "Besides being a liar, you're now acting creepy?"

His brows slammed down. "Excuse me?"

"Watching me dancing. That's creepy."

"I sent you my energy. I let you know I was here."

So that had been him. I hugged my jacket tight. "But how long were you watching me before you did?"

He glanced to his feet before meeting my gaze again and answering, "A couple of minutes."

"Creepy," I said through gritted teeth. By Saint Sara-la-Kali, why didn't he look like a creep? His tall frame in dark pants and tunic and a suede jacket, and his gorgeous face, he looked more like a model ready to march down the catwalk.

Shame he wasn't my model and never would be. Stilling myself, I took three steps toward the door, toward him, but he didn't move. "Aren't you going to let me pass?"

Artan let out a long breath. "I would rather you granted me a moment and talked to me."

I sighed. "How many times do we have to go through this? There's nothing you have to say that I want to hear. Please, let me pass."

He advanced a step toward me. "I can't, Mirella. I can't let you pass. I can't let you go."

"You're engaged, for goodness sake! You should respect me, respect your fiancée, and stay the hell away from me!" I marched past him, but he groaned and caught my wrist. He pulled me back and into him. I hated it; I hated how my body reacted to his, and how his scent filled my nostrils and made me crazy. "Let me go," I whispered, suddenly thinking this was too hard to fight.

"Not until you hear me out, because, damn it, Mirella, you have to hear me out."

The intense shine of his amber eyes wreaked havoc in me. Why, oh why was this so hard to resist?

Mirella, a voice called out inside my mind.

There was only one person who had free access to my mind.

Theron? What is it?

Something big came up. Where are you?

I pushed Artan back. "Excuse me, but Theron is calling me. It's urgent."

Artan dropped his arm and fury fired up his eyes. "That's a lie. An excuse to get away from me."

I shrugged. "So what if it is? As long as it works."

I rushed out of the classroom. The more distance I put

between the two of us, the better. As I had just realized, I was weak when it came to Artan. If he had batted those lashes at me for a moment longer, I would have been a goner. I knew I sometimes was a big bitch and had a short temper and spoke without thinking, but I wasn't a cheater. I would never kiss a guy who belonged to another woman. It had happened before because he had lied to me. Now that I knew, I wouldn't allow it to happen again.

I was halfway through the main square when Artan caught up with me. "What did he say?"

I cocked an eyebrow at him. "I thought you said I was lying."

"Mirella, you don't lie, not like that."

My heart tugged. I did lie. I lied all the time, but he was right, I wouldn't lie about something like this. Theron had inflicted urgency in my mind, and now I couldn't shake that off.

As we walked down the streets leading to the Bellville manor, I glanced up to the graying skies. It was getting colder and colder, and the forecast was for a snowstorm over the weekend. I wasn't ready for that.

We walked by a house with pretty orange lanterns on the porch, and it reminded me of something.

"Do tziganes celebrate Thanksgiving?" We were only a week away from the holiday, but so far, no one had mentioned any celebration.

"No, we don't," Artan said. His voice was calmer now, back to his normal stoic self. "We have another holiday we celebrate where we give thanks and honor our blessings, but it's different from Thanksgiving."

"When is it? What is it?"

He glanced at me, an odd shine to his eyes. "I like when you talk normally to me. You haven't done that in a while."

I buried my hands into the pockets of my jackets. "I'm trying to be normal. After all, I'm stuck as the heart maiden and you're a warrior. Chances are, we'll always be around each other. I would rather we learned how to act like civilized people, then yell all the time."

He let out a long breath. "I like that. I'm not giving up on having a good talk with you yet, but ... you're right. That's better than yelling."

Not sure what to say—or how to feel—I sped up. Probably noticing my hostility was back, Artan didn't push me. In fact, he stayed a step back the entire way.

Theron opened the door of the Bellville manor for us and narrowed his eyes at Artan. "What are you doing here?"

"He was on duty," I quickly said. Which wasn't a lie. He had dismissed the other warriors and was now acting as my bodyguard. I made a mental note to kindly request he take himself out of my bodyguards rotation schedule. He had to understand that was for the best for both of us. "I felt your conflict. What's up?"

"Here." Theron guided us to the living room where Cora, Rye, and Nico were seated.

Eyes wide, Cora stood when she saw me. "Mirella!"

I approached her. "What's going on?"

"I think ..." A smile overtook her lips. "I think my family is still alive."

6

____

I BLINKED. "WHAT?"

"I know," Cora said. "I know it sounds crazy, but I'm sure. I mean, I think I'm sure." She lifted her trembling hands and showed me the envelope she was holding. "I received this letter this morning."

I picked up the envelope and pulled the letter out. Wary, I unfolded the white paper and stared at the symbols filling the page. "What is this?"

"A code!" Cora was scaring me. I had never seen her this excited before. "When I was little, my father and I used to write in code. It was for fun at first, but when I became a warrior, it served to send secret messages." She pointed to the letter. "This is a secret message!"

"And what does it say?"

"That my family is fine. They have been hiding around where our enclave was, but can't get to Lovell safely because the area is often patrolled by alchemists. They've tried several times. They need help coming here."

I frowned. "And how did they know where to find you?"

"My father knew we were meeting Bellville."

I glanced to Rye and Nico. The two men looked tense, suspicious, as if this was too good to be true. I returned my eyes to Cora. "Cora, you know this could be a trap, right?"

"I know. I thought of that, but the alchemists couldn't know our secret code. Even if they had my father, he would never reveal our code." She snatched the letter from my hands. "This is real. See this?" She pointed to the corner of the page. "This is my father's signature. And this." She pointed to another corner. "This is the date. It's from a week ago." She showed me a big, big smile. "He's alive, Mi. They all are."

It didn't make sense. If they were still alive, why hadn't this letter come sooner, like three years ago? Even if they were surrounded by alchemists, I was sure they could have found to contact Cora sooner.

"What do you two think?" I asked Rye and Nico. As members of the same enclave, their emotions were probably all over the place too.

Rye sighed. "I don't know. I want to believe Cora. If she says that's her father's letter, then I believe that." Which meant he didn't truly believe it.

"I think it's a trap," Nico said, his voice tight. "We all saw the attack, the enclave burning." He gestured to Theron. "You went there after and saw the destruction and searched the place. No one survived."

"But they could have left by the time Theron got there," Cora retorted. "They were already running from the alchemists. Surely, they didn't think someone would go back there to look for them."

"I don't know," Rye muttered.

Nico raised his hands. "Whatever you're planning on doing, I'm out. I can't stand any more heartbreak."

"But what if—"

"I don't care, Cora!" Nico cut her off. "I didn't only lose my family that day. I was kidnapped, tortured, and betrayed by my brother." My breath caught. I thought I knew all the details about the attack, but apparently, I didn't. They had never mentioned Nico being captured before. And betrayed by his brother? That was horrible. "I can't go through the hope of finding family and friends, just to have my soul ripped from me again." Tears filled his eyes. "I'm out."

Nico turned stomped out of the living room.

I wanted to ask what had happened, but I didn't want to pry. The Band-Aid had been ripped from the wound, and I didn't want to make it hemorrhage.

After a moment of shock, when everyone was in silence, Theron spoke up. "I did go back there after, and what I told you guys then still holds true. I could never forget what I saw. But I searched the entire enclave, and the immediate forest surrounding it, and didn't find anyone." Cora's shoulders deflated. "But ... that doesn't mean you're wrong, Cora." She perked up again. "If, and I really mean if, there were any survivors, they could have gotten away. If they were good and covering their tracks, I could have missed them."

"See?" Cora turned to me. "This isn't a coincidence."

"If I may say something," Artan said from behind me, startling me. I had forgotten he had come with me. I stepped to the side and looked at him. "From my point of view, this is a trap."

Cora narrowed her eyes. "All right, let's go with the trap thing. Why would alchemists bother sending bait to catch three tziganes from another state? There are plenty of tziganes near the old enclave."

"You have a point there," Rye said. "This seems too elaborate to catch three tziganes."

I eyed Theron. He shrugged at me. I frowned. "All right, let's say this isn't a trap. Why did you call me?"

"Because I don't think the elder council will let the three of us go to check it," Cora said. "Now, if you said you wanted to go with us, they might agree with it."

I gaped at her.

Artan stiffened. "Are you saying you want to waltz into a potential trap with the heart maiden?"

"It isn't a trap," Cora snapped.

"Cora," I started. "You are wrong. The council and I argue all the time. If I tell them I want to go with you to your old enclave to check for survivors, they will laugh in my face. They will never let us go."

"Then we sneak out," she suggested. Her eyes shone with desperation.

"That is *not* an option," Artan said, his voice firm.

"I'm with Artan on that one," Theron said. "Sneaking out would be worse. If we do this, then we gotta be smart and bring an entire team."

"If we do this?" Artan asked with a bite. "We are *not* doing this."

Cora grabbed my hands. "Please, Mi. Even if it's a trap, I have to find out. Why are these alchemists trying to trick us? There must be a reason. And if it's a trap, then we take them down."

"I don't know," I whispered.

She squeezed my hands. "Mi, please ... put yourself in my shoes. This is my family. My father, my mother, my brother.

Maybe even more tziganes from my enclave. What if it was *your* family? Your mother? Or Ellie? You would go check it out, even if there was a chance you were walking into a trap."

Damn it, she was right. I would. For my mother, for Ellie, hell, for any of my friends, I would gladly walk into a trap if that meant having a chance to find the truth, to find out what truly happened, and hopefully save them.

I squeezed her hand back. "Okay. Let's talk to the council."

7

———

THE COUNCIL EITHER PRETENDED TO BE TOO BUSY, OR THEY really were, because after I requested an important meeting with them, it took them an entire day to get back to me. Meanwhile, Cora was having a meltdown, saying we couldn't waste more time. We had to go now.

"Calm down, Cora," Rye repeated every five minutes. "They survived three years without our help. They can survive three more days."

That only went so far. A minute later, she was freaking out again. As for Nico, he hid in his bedroom and refused to talk to any of us. Cora was hurt by his actions, but I understood. After all they had suffered, was it worth putting themselves through more suffering? If it were a trap, the hope that now filled their hearts would become unbearable pain.

But worse than Nico's behavior was Artan's. He was adamant this was a bad idea, and even if the others went on this mission, I shouldn't go.

"You're the heart maiden, Mirella!" he argued. "That

means too much. You can't just go on missions and risk your life."

I ignored him. Hadn't we just agreed to try to get along? He was driving me crazy.

At the appointed time, I waited by the door of the elder council's room with my friends—Cora, Rye, Theron, and Artan. Five minutes after the agreed time, Cora was ready to bang on the door.

Rye wrapped an arm around her shoulders and kept her back. "It's fine, Cora. We'll meet with them soon."

Almost twenty minutes later, the doors were open from the inside, and we were invited in. As we marched to the front of the curved table, the elders talked among themselves, as if we didn't exist.

Irritation began deep in my stomach. Lashing out would only make things worse, so I took a deep breath before doing anything.

"I have a request," I said.

The members of the council finally acknowledged me and started quieting down.

Darcy and Oscar—the *rom baro*, her son, and Artan's father—sat in the center of the curved table, like the king and queen of the enclave.

Oscar glanced at his son standing to my left, then to me. "My dear heart maiden, what is your request?"

I held my chin high. "My friends and I would like your permission to go on a mission." Technically, Theron, Cora, and Rye didn't need the elder council's permission to do anything. Not yet. I was sure the longer they stayed within Lovell's walls, the less Bellville they would be. But they needed more than three warriors for this mission. And since I was the heart maiden and Artan was loyal to this enclave, I had to jump through hoops and walk on a tightrope, or in other words, ask the council's permission before I could sneeze. If I wanted to go on a mission not related to the heart flower? I better be okay with kneeling and begging.

I thought the elder council would jump at the word mission, thinking I had found another heart flower already, but they all seemed eerily calm.

"And what is this mission about?" Oscar asked.

Cora stepped up. "I think my family is alive."

Whispers grew within the council.

"What?" Darcy snapped. "That's preposterous. Your enclave was destroyed three years ago, and your family too." I winced with Darcy's cold tone and callous words. I didn't dare look at Cora for her reaction. "They can't be alive."

"But I think they are." She waved the envelope in her hand. "I think they must have gotten away and hid. And now, they are finally able to contact us." She gestured to Rye, standing behind her.

"You're Bellville," Darcy said. "You don't have to ask us permission for a mission. If you so insist, you can get your warriors and go." Darcy turned her eyes to me. "Now tell me, why are you here?"

What did she mean? "I'm going with them."

The whispers became loud arguments.

Darcy steepled her fingers over the table. "Unless you have sensed a heart flower, you're not allowed to go on missions."

I gritted my teeth. If that was how she wanted to play. "I didn't sense a heart flower, but Damara can communicate with me."

The room quieted with a gasp. Even my friends stared at me as if I had grown another head. This was the first time they were hearing about this. Well, me too, because I was lying. If I didn't come up with something good, the council would lock me in my princess tower and nor prince nor dragon would be able to rescue me.

"H-how is that possible?" Oscar finally asked.

"What did she want?" was Darcy's question.

"I don't know how it's possible," I said. There had never been two heart maidens at once, not that we knew of. Unless the council was hiding that from me, too. And so far only the council and my friends knew about that. It had been the council's order to keep that information from the rest of the enclave, so as not to create panic. It kind of made sense, though it saddened me, because once more, we were all depending on lies. I shrugged. "Maybe it's a connection between heart maidens? There's no documentation, so we're in uncharted territory. But she reached out to me. She now knows where the next heart flower is. She showed it to me. And coincidentally ..." Gosh, I hoped they bought this. "It's close to Cora's old enclave."

Darcy and Oscar exchanged a heated look.

"If that's true," Darcy started, her tone laced with suspicion. "What's your plan?"

"Get together a team and go check it out."

"It sounds like a trap," Oscar said.

"I know, but what other choice do we have?" I held on to Cora's tactic when trying to convince us of going with her. "Even if it's a trap, we can't risk *not* checking it out. If a new heart flower shows up, it's better to be close when it does. If Damara turns up, it'll be our chance to capture her. And if she's lying and there's no flower, we take this opportunity to get to her." So far, the council hadn't decided what to do about Damara. If they had, they hadn't told me. Some were in favor of killing her on the spot, while others wanted to bring her in alive and question her. I was sure they were curious about how she managed to stay alive for over two hundred years. But how could we capture her alive? Unless the council had some hidden weapon, I wasn't sure I could go head-to-head with her like that. "And, while we wait for the flower to show up, or Damara, we search Cora's enclave."

The elders turned to each other and talked among themselves as if we weren't there.

"I don't like that idea."

"It's too risky."

"I'm sure it's a trap. Damara wants to steal Mirella's powers."

"We can't afford that."

"We've lived without a heart flower for years. The heart maiden just found one. We can wait for the next one."

"She was there when I found the last one," I argued, my voice louder so they would hear me. They all turned to me. "And she'll be there when I find the next one. It's just a matter of when."

"Then we wait," Dika said. As one of the oldest members of the council, her voice had weight. "You need more training."

A wave of frustration rolled through me. Who were these pompous old tziganes to talk to me like that? I was their salvation. Without me, they didn't have anything.

I stepped forward, intent on giving them a piece of my mind, when Darcy lifted her hand and everyone looked at her.

"It's risky," she started. "It sounds like a trap, but I agree with you, Mirella." I gaped at her, sure I couldn't be hearing her right. "We have to be prepared for a fight. Mirella against Damara. And if there happens to be a flower there, then we should take the opportunity to retrieve it."

"Are you suggesting we kill Damara?" Artan asked, his body tense beside mine.

Darcy nodded her chin once. "Well, if we had a way to capture her alive and contain her while we question her, that would be best, but since it seems she's too strong for us, it might be best to kill her if you don't have a choice. The sooner she's gone, the safer our heart maiden will be."

I swallowed, reminding myself Darcy was speaking like that because she cared about my powers, about my ability, about finding the flowers the tziganes so desperately needed to live, not because she cared about *me*.

Either way, this was all a lie. There was no flower; Damara hadn't contacted me. This was all a lie so they would allow me to go with Cora and the others.

Again, the council talked among themselves, but in hushed tones this time, so we couldn't hear what they were saying.

Finally, after a long, tense moment, Oscar stood from his chair. "Mirella, you're allowed to go with Cora and Rye to check out their enclave, but we have demands."

I braced myself. "Which are?"

"Artan will be team leader, and you'll obey his every word," Oscar said. I stiffened, hoping nobody noticed how uneasy that order made me. "Your main focus is finding the flower and Damara. Going to the enclave is second, and you'll only go if the team leader thinks it's safe. You'll take a team with you." He looked at his son. "I trust you to choose the team, Artan." He returned his eyes to me. "If you encounter Damara, you fight her, and with the help of the team, kill her."

I swallowed.

Killing was still a strong word for me. If I could help it, I would never kill anyone. Unfortunately, that seemed like it was out of question as long as I was the heart maiden.

Darcy added, "And come back safe."

"Do you understand?" Oscar asked.

I felt like a soldier answering to my superior. "Yes, I understand."

"Then get your team ready, prepare for the mission, and you're allowed to leave tomorrow morning," Oscar said. "Dismissed."

Artan was the first to turn around and march out of the room. Theron, Cora, Rye, and I followed him. As soon as the doors closed behind us, the four of them spun on me.

"What the hell was that about Damara and the heart flower?" Theron asked, his eyes narrowed.

I put my finger over my lips. "Shhh. It's a lie."

"W-what?" Artan asked, visibly appalled.

"I had to lie, otherwise they wouldn't let us go."

"But they are right," he snapped. "This mission is dangerous. You should stay while we go."

"I want to go."

"But—"

"Artan, stop," I cut him off, raising my voice. "If you're gonna be a pain in the ass, then please, let Theron be team leader and stay behind, because I'm not gonna be able to deal with your attitude." His eyes widened. "Now, if you're willing to listen to me, I have a team already chosen."

Theron let out a chuckle. "Way to go."

Cora beamed. "*Nais tuke*. I feel bad you had to lie, but only a little bit. I'm glad you're coming with me."

"Me too." I returned her smile, though mine was forced. I was too frustrated with a certain warrior to have it be true. "Now, let's get ready for our mission."

8

———

EVEN CHOOSING THE TEAM WAS A PROBLEM. ARTAN PRACTICALLY ignored my list, and came up with a different one. After a lot of argument, we found a midway: Cora, Rye, Theron, Ramon, Sloan, Tomas, Ryane, Ellie, Artan, Felix, and me. Of course, we also argued about Ellie and the lion, but I was adamant. Ellie was my best friend and had to come, and Felix was my bodyguard.

"He betrayed us on the last mission," Artan retorted.

"He was under Damara's spell," I objected.

"She could put him under her spell again."

"She won't be there."

At least, I hoped she wouldn't. I didn't think I was ready to face her again so soon. Regardless, Felix and I had worked on his mental defense, and now he could sense if she tried to gain control of his mind again.

In the end, our group had eight warriors, one magical lion, two magic users, and a *gadjo*. I thought we were pretty well equipped for any situation we might encounter.

As expected, I barely slept the previous night. By 4 a.m., I had already showered and dressed in the warriors' uniforms and ready to go. My mother came downstairs around five thirty and prepared breakfast for me.

Her hands shook as she poured tea into my mug. "I wish you weren't going."

I frowned. "I thought you liked that I'm the heart maiden. That it's an honor."

She raised her hard eyes at me. "You think you can lie to me? I know Damara hasn't reached out to you, and there is no heart flower. You're only lying to the council so you can go."

"How ...?"

"By Saint Sara-la-Kali, I'm your mother. I can sense you like no one else can."

I thought of a handful of events in the past when I was a teenager and lied to her. Did she always know about it back then? If she did, why didn't she say anything? Just so I wouldn't find out about our magic?

That didn't matter now. What mattered was that she didn't tell the elder council. "If you know, why aren't you arguing with me?"

She sighed. "Because I know you. No matter what I say, you'll do whatever you want, whenever you want. When I say no, that's when you feel most compelled to really do it."

Well, she had me there.

I reached out and cradled her hands in mine. "Mom, it'll be fine."

"Everyone thinks it's a trap."

"I know, and that's why we have eight warriors on our team. Plus Felix. We'll be fine."

"You never know."

I chuckled. "Be optimistic for once. Pray to Saint Sarah-la-Kali if you want. Think positive. It'll all work out, okay?"

She grunted and pulled her hands from mine. She grumbled under her breath as she returned to her chores around the kitchen. When it was time for me to go, she gave me a quick kiss and hug, then pushed me out the door before I could see her crying.

Dressed in his best warrior uniform and holding a heavy duffel bag in his hands, Artan was waiting for me on the street.

"I thought she would cling to you and beg you not to go," he said.

I started walking toward the main entrance. "She wants to, so instead, she pushed me away. You can bet she's crying now."

Artan fell into step with me. "Well, she knows this is a crazy mission."

I closed my eyes for a moment and took a deep breath before I barked at him. He was getting on my nerves, and I was bound to spend a lot of time with him over the next few days. If I killed him now, our mission was over.

So I reigned in my rage and didn't answer him.

When we got to the enclave's main entrance, Cora, Rye, Theron, and Ramon were already by the van, ready to go. Soon after, Sloan, Tomas, and Ryane arrived. Lastly, Felix appeared. He projected an image in my mind of Sheila opening his cage so he could come to us.

Even though it would have been faster to fly, there was no way we could go through security check with our weapons and elixirs. We thought about renting a smaller airplane, but we doubted the council would approve that kind of expense. So, even though it would take us about nine hours, we had to drive. The van seated fifteen people, but because of Felix and his huge size, we were getting rid of one row for him. As expected, Artan took the wheel. His cousin, Sloan, sat in the passenger seat beside him. In the second row sat Cora, Rye, and Ramon. Tomas and Ryane occupied the third row. And Theron and I sat in the fourth row—we saved an empty seat for Ellie with us. Finally, Felix was in the back along with most of our bags.

Artan glanced back. "Everyone ready?"

Cora practically jumped up and down on her seat. "Ready!" Since receiving the letter with the code, she was too eager, too jumpy. So unlike her usual stoic warrior self. But I guess if I received a letter like that, I would have changed a little bit, too. I would be going crazy until I found out the truth.

"Then let's go." Artan started the engine, put on some lovely old school flamenco song on the speakers, and drove out of the enclave.

I texted Ellie, knowing we were on our way to pick her up.

Ellie: *I'm ready!*

I smiled. Theron glanced at my phone and smiled, too. I guess he was eager to spend some time away from the enclave with her. I was quite happy for the two of them, too.

"What's going on with you?" I asked him in a low voice.

His grin widened. "I'm still figuring it out myself."

"But you like her?"

He turned those dark eyes to me. "I do." Then his jaw hardened. "But she's a *gadjo*."

"Who cares? You like her. That's all that matters."

"I wish it were that simple. She'll never be accepted as one of our own. Even my *dat* and my *puri daj* won't accept her as my partner. I know that."

I nudged him with my elbow. "Hey. You're the great warrior Theron. The one with the permanent cocky smile."

He loosened up, and one of the corner of his lips curled up in his trademark grin. "Don't let that get you down. Whatever happens, I'm on your side. If things get bad, I'll intervene."

"And what is the great heart maiden going to do to help us?"

"I know the elder council seems to have chips on their shoulders when it comes to me—believe me, I have one with them too—but the truth is, they need me. If I put my foot down and tell them how it's gonna be or I won't do whatever they want, they will agree. You'll see."

He let out a low chuckle. "I believe you."

We fell silent for the rest of the ride. As agreed, Ellie was waiting for us in front of her dorm building, a backpack slung over shoulder. She was wearing jeans, boots, and a heavy wool coat, but once she had a chance, she would change into the warrior's uniform I had brought for her. Even if she wasn't going to fight, the uniform had magical properties and was more than just armor—it protected against the cold too.

"Hi!" she called as she hopped inside the van and weaved to the back. On purpose, I scooted to the end of the seat, so she could sit between Theron and me.

"Hey you," I said as she took her place.

Artan spied us through the rearview mirror. "Ready?"

Ellie reached for the seat belt. "Ready!"

Theron twisted and grabbed the seat belt from Ellie. "Here. I'll help you."

Her cheeks turned red. "Thanks."

"All right," Artan called out, and he exited the campus parking lot. "Sit tight, everyone. This trip will be long."

I forced a yawn and, using my jacket as pillow, leaned against the window. "I didn't sleep well, so I'm gonna try to take a nap." That was code for I'm-gonna-leave-you-two-alone-so-enjoy and Ellie knew it.

She showed me a soft grin before turning back to Theron and starting a conversation with him.

I put in my earbuds and pressed play on a new reggaeton song I was into, then closed my eyes and pretended to sleep. Meanwhile, Ellie scooted an inch closer to Theron.

My job here was done.

To my surprise, I ended up sleeping for real. Maybe it was the movement of the van, or the lull of the song playing in my earbuds, but I actually slept. Although, my dream was confusing and when I woke up, I felt uneasy.

In my dream, I had seen alchemists descending upon Cora's enclave and setting the houses on fire. The screams of tziganes locked inside the houses filled my head.

What a ridiculous dream. Alchemists would never kill tziganes like that. Instead, they would have taken the tziganes, even if dead, so they could harvest their blood.

I shuddered and curled into my corner, pushing those thoughts away. The van was quiet and everyone was either sleeping or messing with their phones. I looked out to the interstate. The sun was high in the sky, which meant I had slept for a couple of hours. Good. For someone who hadn't been sleeping well, each nap counted.

Another few minutes passed until Artan steered the van off the road and into a gas station.

"What happened?" Sloan asked.

"Gas," Artan said. "The van's power is impressive, but it consumes gas like it is water."

"Good," Ryane said from the middle of the van. "I need to stretch my legs."

As he slowed down and parked the van beside the gas pump, I noticed the place looked abandoned. There were no other cars, no other customers. If the lights on the doors of the small convenience store hadn't been on and we couldn't see a young man behind the counter inside, I would have thought the gas station was closed.

Everyone jumped out of the van as soon as Artan turned the engine off. We all went to the bathroom, then grabbed water and some snacks while Artan filled the tank.

I stopped by the van's back doors and glanced around. "There's no one around, right?"

Artan stepped to the side of the van. "It seems it's just the guy working here. Why?"

"Because ..." I opened the back doors. Felix jumped out and brushed his side on my legs. The top of his head came to my chest and his powerful legs were twice as thick as mine. I was sure if anyone saw him, they would have a heart attack. Even when he behaved like a big, fluffy cat.

Artan's eyes went wide. "What if the guy sees him?"

I dug my hand in the lion's soft mane. "Then I'll assure him Felix is docile."

With a loud sigh, he shook his head and finished filling the van. "If everyone is ready, we should hit the road."

Ryane tsked. "Give us another five minutes, please."

"Agreed," Cora said. She stretched her arms above her head, then touched her toes. Ryane and Ellie joined her in stretching a little.

Meanwhile, Ramon walked off, grumbling something about wasting time. Rye, Sloan, and Tomas leaned against the van.

Come on, I said in Felix's mind. We walked to the edge of the trees beside the gas station. *Go run a little. Stretch your legs.*

The lion let out a content purr then dashed off into the forest.

I inhaled deeply and rolled my shoulders. We had been on the road for four hours. Even if we traveled nonstop, as was the plan—Theron and Sloan and Rye and Tomas had volunteered to switch with Artan when needed—we wouldn't arrive until that evening. We would be cramped in the van, so I tried enjoying this little break.

Then an image filled my mind: Felix running through the forest.

Running from alchemists.

Panic surged in my chest.

A second later, Felix burst from the trees and let out a loud growl that sent a shiver down my spine.

The lion bumped into my legs, pushing me back. I pushed down the panic and spun on my heels. "Alchemists!" I screamed, running to my friends. "Alchemists are here."

Immediately, my friends formed a line in front of me— Theron joined them after pushing Ellie inside the van. Felix and I stood beside them as the alchemists appeared from the forest.

Over two dozen masked men with shadow swords came at us—but they looked different, with dark red masks instead of black, and their shadow swords had a red blood glow to it. What was going on?

"Shit," Theron muttered as he drew his sword.

"How did they find us?" Artan asked. He hadn't pulled out his sword, but I could feel his magic crackling in the air. He was ready to strike.

"Does it matter?" Sloan barked, holding his sword at his side.

"Agreed," Tomas said. "We worry about that later. Now, we fight."

As if they had rehearsed it, Tomas and Sloan ran out and met the alchemists halfway.

"By Saint Sara-la-Kali," Artan muttered before joining them. Theron and Rye and Ramon joined them. Even Felix leapt toward our enemies.

As primarily magic users, Cora, Ryane, and I stayed back, but we engaged in the battle, too.

The alchemists spread out, attacking each of us in groups of twos or threes. I raised a shield of fire to distract them for a moment. When the shield went down, I had fire bolts in my hands. I threw the bolts at them. One dodged it, the other spun around and got grazed by the fire, and the other fell back as the bolt exploded against his chest.

A few steps to my side, Ryane flung water at our enemies, while Cora sent little rocks at them. She also played with the ground, making big rocks jut out from beneath their feet. With the impact, they flew up for a second before falling hard on their backs.

Another handful of alchemists appeared from the forest.

"What the hell?" someone said.

Before they could reach our group, I channeled more of my magic, and using both hands, brought up a long wall of fire.

"The heart maiden!" one of the alchemists said.

"Get her!" another shouted.

As if my friends were nonexistent, they all turned to me.

I took a couple of steps back. "Crap."

Artan and Theron and Felix ran to my side.

When they were close enough, Theron and Felix lunged at the alchemists, while Artan used his air magic to push them back. I stood by his side, sending fire bolts left and right.

One alchemist dodged our magic and stepped right in front of us, his shadow sword at ready. Artan grabbed my wrist and pulled me behind him, while he drew his sword with his other hand.

Never letting go of me, he fought the alchemist.

From over his shoulder, or from around him, I tried keeping the rest away with my magic, but it seemed like they sprouted from the ground. We took them down, and they either didn't stay down or more came from the edge of the forest.

What was happening?

I jerked against Artan's tight grip. "Let me go," I protested. "I can't fight like this."

He glanced over my shoulder. "I prefer to know you're safe behind me."

Frustration filled my chest along with three hundred other feelings. What the hell was he thinking? I had been training for a couple of months now to be able to protect myself, even if only with my magic. If he kept me from fighting, it would only make it harder.

Finally, I jerked free of his grip and stood by his side, helping him fight our enemies. Artan didn't look happy about it, but he was supposed to protect me, not control me.

I raised a fire shield and pushed it back, like a wave on the ocean, and the alchemists around us retreated so they wouldn't be burned. Calling my magic, I got ready to make the shield longer, wider, so it kept the alchemists away from all my friends, but without warning, it started again. The pain in the back of my skull, stronger than before, and the visions that seemed too vivid to be only dreams, or nightmares.

The pain spread through my head and down my neck. I grunted, falling to my knees. I couldn't distinguish reality from visions as heavy black clouds covered the sky. The alchemists broke the window of our van and pulled a screaming Ellie out. At my side, Felix fell on the pavement, bleeding out. I lifted my hands to use my magic, but I didn't feel it. Not even a trickle of magic inside my veins. Nothing. It was like my magic was gone. The alchemists surrounded me, their shadow swords pointed at my neck. Artan shouted my name. Then the alchemists parted and Damara walked inside the circle. Her lips curled into an evil smile.

Pain blinded me and I fell on the ground, screaming.

9

"Mirella!"

"What's going on?"

"I have no idea."

"I've seen this before."

"Where?"

"At her house the other day. She said she was having pain and visions. Her mother gave her a calming elixir and it stopped."

"Do we have a calming elixir here?"

"No, but I can try using my powers."

"Do it, then."

A cool sensation started in my chest, right above my heart. It seeped into me, and inch by inch, it spread through my veins. When it reached my toes, the cool sensation turned cold, and was getting colder fast.

Snapping out of my daze, I opened my eyes and sat up with a jerk.

Artan was seated on the pavement, with half my body in his lap, and Ryane had her open palms hovering inches from me. The others formed a circle around us and eyed me as if I would burst into fire at any time.

"What happened?" I asked, my voice scratching my throat.

"We should ask you that." Artan's amber eyes locked on mine, worry shining through them. "What was that?"

I averted my gaze. "I ... I don't know."

"Ellie just told us it happened before," Theron said.

I glared at Ellie. Traitor. "It did, but I still have no idea what it is."

"How are you feeling?" Ryane asked.

I thought for a moment—no pain, and the visions were gone. "I feel fine. Normal."

"I'm not great at healing, but I know my powers can be refreshing," she said. "If you want, I can give you some more just to be sure."

I pushed up to my feet. A wave of dizziness assaulted me, but I did my best to keep it in, so they wouldn't all fret about it. "No, I'm good now." While Artan and Ryane stood up too, I looked around. Several bodies of alchemists littered the area. "Did we win?" I asked, taking my friends in. Theron had a nasty red mark on his cheek—it would probably turn purple soon. Sloan had a bandage on his forearm, and Rye had one on his shoulder. The others looked disheveled and sweaty and tired but no apparent injuries. However, there was someone missing. "Where's Ramon?"

Theron's clenched his fists. "That punk ran off to distract a group of alchemists. We have to go after him."

Artan shook his head. "We should separate. Half of us go after Ramon. The other half stays here with Mirella while she recovers."

I gaped at him. "What?"

"We're wasting time," Theron said. "Just choose whoever and let's do it."

"We're not separating," I said, adamant. "I'm fine and I would rather we don't separate."

"But you just had … whatever that was." Artan gestured to the ground where I had just been. "What if it happens again?"

"It won't!" I snapped.

One of his eyebrows cocked up. "How can you be sure?"

"I can't, but I'm fine now. It won't happen again. Not so soon."

"Come on, guys, my brother might need help," Theron insisted.

Artan took a step closer and towered over me. "Fine. But know this. When we're back at Lovell, we're investigating whatever that was."

I lifted my chin and held his hard stare. "Fine." I turned to Theron. "Where to?"

He jerked his chin to the right. "This way."

No matter how much I tried to dodge him, Artan stayed right by my side as we marched into the forest and followed Ramon's trail. On the way, I asked about the guy working at the convenience store.

"Obviously, he saw us," Cora told me. "But Ryane went in and put his mind at ease. She told him to hide."

"He's probably still hiding," Ryane said.

Poor guy. Must have been scared out of his mind when he saw the tziganes and the alchemists fighting. It wasn't a truth easy to swallow.

"Anyone noticed these alchemists are different?"

After a few minutes, I asked into Theron's mind, *Do you have a connection like this with him?*

Not exactly like this, he answered. *Ours is weaker. We can't form words, just images and feelings.*

So like Felix and me.

Yes, something like that.

I frowned, wondering why Theron and I had such a connection. It wasn't the first I thought about it, and even Sheila had admitted it wasn't a normal thing, but since my first magic lessons with Sheila, Theron and I had been able to communicate telepathically.

Is he showing the way? I asked.

Sort of. I think he was caught and drugged, so the few images he showed me were blurred.

Crap. We should go faster, then.

I'm trying.

I sped up, ditching Artan, even for a couple of seconds, until he reached me again, and caught up with Theron. "Just walk faster. The others will do the same."

With an amused half-grin, Theron accelerated. But dodging tree roots and low branches and loose rocks and hills proved to be harder when we tried speeding up. Ryane tripped and scraped her knee, and Ellie scratched her arm on a thorny bush.

"We're almost there," Theron said, loud enough for the entire party to hear.

A couple of minutes later, Felix growled and slowed down.

I placed my hand on his big head. "What happened, boy?"

He pushed an image of darkness descending over the forest and all around us into my mind. A warning. Whatever was in front of us, he sensed it was evil.

"What is it?" Theron asked, knowing well the lion sometimes picked up more than we did.

"Just ... be careful," I said.

Theron slowed down but didn't stop. He climbed down a hill and walked past a thick line of trees. We followed him. Three steps past the tree line, I halted.

A house sat in the middle of the forest.

"What is this?" Cora asked, staring at the odd house.

It was four stories tall and clearly abandoned, judging by the broken windows, fallen siding, missing roof tiles, and the rot taking over the front porch. The vegetation grew around and over it, as if the house were part of the forest. Two large trees had branches reaching inside the house through holes in the wooded sides. The grass was tall and the bushes grew over the porch railing.

Theron looked to the top of the eerie house. "I think Ramon is inside."

"If it were dark now, I would say this is straight out of a horror movie," Ellie said. She scooted closer to Theron.

He placed an arm around her shoulder. "Just stay close to me and you'll be fine."

My heart squeezed as jealousy snaked around my chest. Was that what Artan was trying to do with me? Keep me close to keep me safe? He had done it before, and he had been better at it back then. But that was before I found out he was promised to another girl and started pushing him away.

I shook my head. It didn't matter now. That was all in the past, and I had to let him go.

Closing my eyes, I sent my senses out. I sensed the mold eating the house from below, the dead rats in the crawl space underneath, the ones alive running amok, the rotten wood frame, the dirt and dust covering every inch of the decaying house, but I didn't sense one person inside. No tziganes, no alchemists, no *gadjos*.

I opened my eyes "It's empty."

"I can't sense anyone either," Artan said.

"I know," Theron said. "But something tells me to go in."

Do you see him here? I asked him.

Not exactly, he answered. *Call it brother connection or whatever.*

"We should check it out," Rye spoke up. "Just to be safe."

Beside me, Artan grunted.

I lowered my head before I snapped at him. I couldn't believe I was once attracted to him. Okay, I admit, I still was, but it was different now. Before I was blind. I would have fallen into his arms without questioning anything. Now, besides knowing I couldn't fall into his arms, I would be hesitant to. It was like a mask had been lifted, and I could see his real self now.

"Rye and I will go through the back," Cora said.

Tomas stepped toward the couple. "Me too."

Sloan raised his hand. "Me too."

"Fine," Artan said through gritted teeth. "The rest of us will go through the front. We meet in the middle of the house."

"Sounds good," Rye said.

The four of them marched around the house, while Artan, Theron, Ryane, Ellie, Felix, and I went up the porch steps. The wood creaked under our weight, and I was afraid it would actually break and we would fall into some kind of dungeon.

Artan reached for the broken knob, and I channeled my magic, filling my veins with my fire, ready for battle. He pushed the door open, revealing a large four-story foyer with cracked stone floors and a round wooden staircase with missing steps and half of the rusty railing.

If taken care of, this house could be a beautiful mansion, but why was it sitting in the middle of the forest? It seemed like something out of the Wizard of Oz.

We met with the other group and searched all the rooms on the first floor. Nothing more than dust and broken furniture.

Together, we went up the stairs.

Felix started growling before we reached the second floor's landing.

A couple of dark red spots stained the wooden floors.

"Is that ...?" Ryane asked, her nose wrinkled.

Artan crouched beside it, rubbed his fingertip on a bigger dot, and smelled. "Tzigane blood."

Theron's face paled. "Shit."

A few steps forward, we saw a couple more spots. An archway led to a wide corridor, where we found more blood drops. Holding our breath, we followed the trail to the last room on that floor.

Artan halted at the open door. "What the ...?"

We all crowded behind him, trying to sneak a peek inside.

My stomach turned as I took in the two hospital beds, the low tables with several medical instruments, the metal pole with IV bags and needles. It reminded of when Ellie and I had been tricked by the alchemists months ago. They had tied us to similar beds, and would have taken all of my blood if we hadn't been able to break free and fight our way out.

However, this room was covered in blood. Blood on the floor, blood on the beds, blood on the table.

I pressed a hand over my mouth, trying hard not to think this blood was Ramon's.

Artan examined the blood on the top of a table. "It's fresh. Whatever happened here was less than thirty minutes ago."

My stomach sank. Then ... it could be Ramon?

"He isn't here," Theron said, his voice tight. "Let's keep looking."

The group became eerily quiet as we backtracked to the staircase.

"Third floor?" Artan asked at the base of the stairs.

"Yes." Theron nodded, his neck tense. "Let's search every inch of this place. Even if they aren't here, there must be some clue."

"Just be alert," Artan said. "It's better if—"

A scream echoed through the house.

10

———

"WHAT'S THAT?" ELLIE ASKED, HER VOICE TREMBLING.

"I think ..." Theron reached for the hilt of his sword. "It's Ramon."

Artan pointed to the stairs in front of us. "It's coming from above."

With Artan, Theron, and Felix taking the lead, we all went up the stairs—step by step, breath by breath.

But when a new guttural scream made the hairs on my arms stand on end, Theron lost it and rushed up the stairs, taking three steps at a time.

Artan cursed under his breath but followed him. We all sped up to catch up with Theron and save Ramon. I didn't expect to find him frozen like a block of ice on the fourth-floor landing, staring at the other side of the stairwell.

"What is it?" Cora asked, coming to stand beside Theron.

He didn't need to tell us what it was, though, because we all had already seen. Behind us, the landing led to a corridor with several doors, but across the stairwell, there was another landing with no visible way of reaching it. The only way to get to it was to jump across the stairwell, or fly since it was too far for a normal jump.

However, what made us hesitate wasn't the impossible way to reach it. Ramon was on that second landing. He was strapped to a chair, with several IVs sticking from his arms. Three alchemists either messed with the dozens of potions spread out on the tables around the room or hovered over him, waiting for the complete harvest of his blood.

"What is that?" Sloan asked.

"The symbols?" Rye asked.

"I've never seen them before," Ryane said.

I hadn't even noticed the symbols until they mentioned them, but now that it had been brought to my attention, it was all I could see. Odd symbols drawn in what looked like blood covered the floor around Ramon's chair.

My stomach revolved.

"Let him go!" Theron shouted.

One of the alchemists placed a knife to Ramon's throat. "Stay right there if you want him to live."

Theron fisted his hands. "You—"

Cora placed a hand on his arm. "They are taking his blood. They are gonna kill him anyway."

"She's right," Rye said. "If we attack now, then we have a chance to save him."

Theron didn't need to think twice. As fast as lightning, he grabbed a dagger from the strap around his waist and threw it at the alchemist holding the knife to Ramon's throat. The dagger flew true and pierced the alchemist's neck. The knife clattered to the floor, and the alchemist fell to the ground with a thud.

The battle began all at once.

Artan used his air power to propel Theron then himself

over the stairwell. The two remaining alchemists grabbed vials of potions and elixirs from the tables and threw them at us, causing us to retreat. Alchemists, dozens of them, ran up the stairs and attacked us.

"Where did they come from?" Sloan asked.

"I don't know!" Ryane shouted as she conjured a whip of water.

In the tumult, Ellie ended up on the other side of the room with Cora and Rye and Felix. Worry for her rose in my chest, but I pushed it down, focusing on one matter at a time. And the important one right now was fighting and defeating these alchemists.

My magic awakened and filled my veins, bringing warmth to my skin. I cast fire bolts and threw them at the alchemists pouring from the stairs.

"That's the heart maiden!" one alchemist shouted.

Like before, most of the alchemists turned to me. They rushed at me. Retreating a few steps, I raised a wall of fire. A couple of alchemists ran into it and screamed as my fire burned them. A smarter one pulled out a vial from his pocket and threw it at the wall. The fire crackled then sizzled. My wall crumbled like ashes.

On instinct, I retreated a couple of steps while throwing more bolts at the alchemists, but that only slowed them down. I was cornered in a large room with a broken window. There was another door on the other side of the room. I ran to it, tried to open it, but it was locked.

"Nowhere to run now, heart maiden," one alchemist called, his dark eyes fixed on mine. A shiver ran up my spine. I had seen them without the masks covering the lower part of their faces before. They looked like monsters with blackened mouths and dark eyes.

I glanced to the window. I preferred to throw myself from the fourth floor and hope I only broke a leg in the fall rather than being caught by alchemists.

As I was trying to convince myself to jump, another idea came to mind.

I turned my hand and conjured my fire. It snaked out from my palm, down my arm, across my torso, down my legs. Like a long, thick snake, the fire weaved to the floor. With suspicious eyes, the alchemists turned toward my snake.

"What is that?" one asked, pointing his red-shadow sword at it.

One corner of my lips turned up as the snake stretched, and in the blink of an eye, it surrounded the alchemists. I lifted my hands, and the fire jutted upward, locking my enemies in a fire circle.

One alchemist touched the fire, probably thinking about walking through it, but he hissed and retracted his hand. "Little bitch."

Sword in hand, Artan burst into the room. "Oh," he said, staring at my fire cage in the middle of the room. "That's ... good job." He smiled at me.

His smile made my heart squeeze in pain.

Although I fought it, I smiled back at him. "Thanks."

He marched to me. "I don't know how, but alchemists haven't stopped coming and—"

"They won't stop coming," one alchemist said.

Artan glared at the man.

I reached for Artan, bringing his attention to me before he wasted more time with the alchemists. "And?"

"We need to go now before we can't fight anymore."

"What about Ramon?"

"Theron and Ellie are taking him out now." He reached for my hand. "Come on."

We made it to the door, but more alchemists pushed in. Artan pulled me to the back of the room to the other door.

"That's locked," I said.

He sent a blast of air to the door. It trembled with the powerful wind, but stayed firm on its hinges.

The alchemists surrounded us, their red-shadow swords pointed at our chest.

"Hand us the heart maiden and no harm will come to you," one alchemist said.

Artan snorted. "You can do whatever you want with me, but I'll never let you touch her."

Dropping my hand, Artan put down his foot firmly on the floor and threw his palms out. A strong gust of wind blew the alchemists several feet away. Artan grabbed my arm and tugged me. "Ready?"

"For?"

He wrapped his arms around my waist and pulled me to him. My hands on his shoulders, I gasped. I looked up at him, at his amber eyes fixed on mine. His lips turned up. "To fly."

"Wha—?"

He jumped.

I clung to him and swallowed a scream as we flew out the window. A moment later, we landed like feathers on the ground below.

I gave a step back, but my trembling legs betrayed me and I almost fell in the tall grass. Artan's hands supported my elbows.

"Careful," he said, his voice soft. I hadn't seen this unguarded look, this easy smile, heard this calm voice, felt his warm touch in weeks. I had missed it.

But he wasn't mine to be missed.

I pushed away. "I'm okay."

Artan frowned.

"Hey, you two," Sloan cried from the front of the house. "Let's go!"

Without another word, Artan and I rushed toward our friends as they ran out of the house. Ramon's arms were slung around Theron's and Rye's shoulders, and Ellie hovered around them, as if she could catch him in case he fell.

I counted. One. Three. Five. Nine. Plus Felix and me. We were all here.

"Get them!" I heard a shout from the house, but I didn't dare turn to look. It could only be alchemists coming for us.

"Faster!" Artan ordered from beside me. "We need to move faster, or they will be upon us in a minute."

Not that I liked killing, in fact I avoided it at all costs, but why couldn't we just stop and take them down? Then, we could take our time in leaving. And we could actually take a good look at Ramon and tend to his wounds.

But when I finally gave in and glanced back, the air fled my lungs. Another two dozen alchemists raced from the house toward us.

"I don't understand," I said, pushing harder and trying to speed up. "Where are they coming from?"

"Right?" Cora asked from my right. "That's too many alchemists."

"And they weren't there when we first entered the house," Rye reminded us.

True.

Then how the hell were there so many? And why were they different from the usual alchemists we faced?

It didn't matter. As long as we could outrun them, reach our van, and leave this place, it didn't matter.

Felix sent an image of the alchemists rushing toward us in my mind, filled with his rising panic and fury. A moment later, Artan yelled, "Sloan, with me."

They slowed down and turned toward the alchemists.

I slowed down, too.

The mass of alchemists reached the cousins.

"What are you doing?" I cried. If they didn't keep running, they would be engulfed and killed.

"Just go," Artan said. "It's an order."

An order my ass.

"Cora, help me," I yelled.

She appeared by my side. "What?"

"This is your playground." I gestured toward the ground. "Do whatever you need to slow the alchemists down. I'm going to help Artan and Sloan. Ready?"

She nodded once. "Always."

Cora lifted her hands. The ground shook as rocks jutted out, slamming into the alchemists. They either fell over it, or had to slow down to go around them.

"Keep doing that," I said, running to Artan and Sloan.

Sloan used his sword to contain the crowd, while Artan used his magic as well as his weapon. I skidded to a halt behind them and sent out little fire snakes out. They slithered along the forest floor until they were under the alchemist. Then, they snaked up their legs, and when they reached their chests, they exploded into fire. I didn't use enough energy to kill them, but I was sure they would get knocked out and wake up with a pretty nasty burn mark.

One by one, the alchemists went down, bitten by my fire snakes.

"Nice," Sloan said, retreating from the fallen alchemists.

Artan watched me with pride shining in his eyes. "Pretty good."

A smile tugged at the corner of my lips, but it didn't break through. More alchemists raced toward us.

"What the crap?" I asked, confused. "Where are they coming from?"

Artan caught my hand. "It doesn't matter. Run."

We took two steps before vines sprouted from the ground, forming green cages and locking us in.

I spied through the cracks in the entwined vines—everyone, even the rest of my friends and the alchemists had been caught by the vines.

"What—?" Sloan's words died on the tip of his tongue.

A new shape took form in front of us.

Woman shaped body, skin like bark, jet black hair that went down to her ankles, white dress flowing as if caught in a breeze.

I gasped. "Muma Padurii."

"We meet again, heart maiden." Her voice was raspy, resembling nails scratching on wood. I suppressed a shudder. She looked around with her depthless black eyes. "What are you doing to my forest?"

"It isn't our fault!" I said, trying to stay calm. If I could only convince her, I was sure she could help us here. "We were at a rest stop with no intentions of coming inside the forest when alchemists attacked us. They took our friend, so we had to come after him."

Her eyes narrowed. "You mean the evil beings inhabiting that house?"

"You know about them?"

"So they are alchemists. Interesting."

"What do you mean?"

"That house simply showed up a few months ago. It squashed a good portion of my forest. I tried to get a read on it, but somehow, it can keep my magic out."

Which reminded me ... "We tried sensing it before, and it was empty. But once we went in, we saw alchemists with our friend. And then more and more showed up."

"They are masking their presence. I know there are many of them inside, but I can never see or sense them." She looked around. "But now many of them are out here."

This was my chance. "You can stop them now. Look, they've destroyed your forest." I pointed to the marks of swords on tree trunks, and broken branches.

She glared at me. "You're not off the hook, heart maiden. You've been fighting in this forest and hurting my plants like them."

"But that's only because they are after us." I paused. "You've got all of us in your vine-cages now. Just release my friends and me, and we'll leave peacefully, without harming your forest any longer. And then you can do whatever you want with the alchemists."

"Tempting," Muma purred.

"You've got nothing to lose."

She clicked her tongue. "All right, I'll do it, but on one condition."

I sucked in a sharp breath. Of course there was a condition. "What is it?"

"Next time I see you damaging my forest, even if you're not at fault, I'm taking my revenge."

I gulped. Well, I would never damage the forest on purpose. Hopefully, I would never damage it at all.

Artan grabbed my arm and whispered, "You can't promise

that. There will be times when we're after the heart flower and we'll fight. In the forest."

"That is in the future. This is now. I'll take my chances." I jerked my arm free from his grip and turned to Muma. "Deal."

She offered me a smile with her black sharp teeth. The vines retreated, disappearing into the ground as if they had never been there. "Off you go."

I looked back. The alchemists were still locked within the vines. She had kept her promise.

"Thank you." I glanced to Artan and Sloan. "Let's go."

Without hesitating, we ran off.

About thirty yards to our right, Cora appeared from among the trees, her face pale. "What was that?"

"I'll explain later," I told her. "Just go."

We kept running until we reached the rest of our friends almost at the edge of the forest.

"What was that?" Ryane asked when she saw us approaching.

Theron looked at me from over Ramon's drooped head. "Let me guess, it was Muma."

I nodded. "The one and only."

Ellie shuddered. "Oh my God, I hate that crazy woman."

"All right," Artan said, his tone firmer than it had been in the last few hours. "We can talk and argue and complain more later. We have to get out of here."

The group fell silent as we marched out of the forest and jumped into our van. Without waiting for everyone to sit down and buckle up, Artan started the engine and pulled out of the gas station.

Felix had been the first inside, and he scooted to a corner as if knowing we needed space now, but thankfully, the van was big enough and we were able to lay Ramon down in one row by himself. Ryane and Theron knelt on the van's floor beside him. Ryane used her water magic to calm and heal him, while Theron bandage the wounds caused by the needles that had been stuck in his arms.

"Get off me," Ramon rasped, trying to get up.

Theron pushed him down. "Just stay quiet, man, and let us do our thing."

Ramon groaned. "Let me sit up at least." Even though he looked terribly weak, he straightened. Ryane sat to his left and Theron on his right.

Five minutes later, Ryane hissed. "I feel something ..." She retreated her hands. "There's something wrong."

Theron finished up the last bandage. "What do you mean?"

"I don't know," she said, her voice low. Worried.

Theron looked at Ramon. "What are you feeling?"

Ramon blinked at Theron. "I don't ..." His head drooped. "I don't know."

All of a sudden, Ramon rolled to the floor of the van, trembling from head to toe.

11

THERON SCOOTED TO THE END OF THE ROW AND KNELT BESIDE his brother, trying to hold him down. "What's happening?"

Eyes wide, Ryane threw her hands out. "I don't know!"

"Heal him," Theron barked.

"I'm trying! But I'm not a full scale healer. I can't heal him properly, especially since we don't know what exactly is going on."

Holding the seat in front of me, I crossed to Ellie and crouched beside Theron. "Arguing won't help right now. Let's try to keep a cool head and think this through."

Theron glared at me. "Look who is talking. Miss do-it-first-think-about-it-later." I winced at the bite in his words. He exhaled deeply and ran a hand through his messy hair. "Sorry. I didn't mean it."

"I know," I muttered. Although, that didn't mean it didn't hurt. For his sake, I would disregard it for now. "There must be something we can do."

Ryane pushed more of her magic into Ramon, but it only went so far. "I ... I feel him fading away."

"What do you mean?" Theron asked, his voice breaking.

"I'm no expert, but I think he's dying."

Theron's face paled. "No."

"Let me try." I put my hands on Ramon's chest and sent him some of my fire and warmth. I had been able to help Cora. I hoped it worked now, too. A moment later, Ramon's tremors lessened, but only a little.

Ryane checked his pulse. "It's not enough. We need something more."

Theron's shoulders rolled back and his eyes bulged. "I might have something." He reached for a leather satchel under the seat. "Before we left the house, I got some of the alchemists' potions and a couple of books."

The van jerked to the side as Artan shouted, "Whaaat?"

Only Artan spoke, but he gave voice to everyone's thoughts.

Then Sloan spied over the back of his seat. "Why did you do that?"

"Those alchemists looked different, with those red masks and red shadow swords. Besides, I have never seen those symbols or odd-looking potions. I thought we could study them." He paused. "For fighting purposes."

"You—"

Ryane cut her brother off. "We can argue about that later. Artan, focus on driving."

Unfortunately, she was right. We couldn't stop and risk being found again. "Right now, let's take a look in these books and see if we can find a healing potion." She extended her hand to Theron.

He passed a book to her, another one to Sloan, and he opened the third one. Meanwhile, the tension inside the van increased tenfold, and I tried to keep Ramon from hurting himself with my fire.

They flipped through the leather-bound books furiously. I got a glimpse of a few pages and the odd symbols were all over. I was actually glad Theron had snatched these. It would be interesting to study these alchemists and find out how different from the normal ones they were.

"I think I found something," Theron said, opening the book wide. "It's not clear, but this potion will give the person enhanced senses and super healing."

Cora spied over the seat. "What else does it say?"

Theron flipped the page, then came back to the first one. "Nothing. There are no warnings or side effects listed."

"There's gotta be a catch," Rye said in a low voice.

"It looks too easy," Tomas added.

"We don't have much of a choice here," Theron said.

"Just for the record, I'm against it," Artan said from the front. "We aren't sure if those books are authentic, or if those potions are poisonous."

"Theron," Ryane called. "You need to make a decision. We're losing him."

Lips pressed into a thin line, Theron reached inside the satchel and looked for the potion. By Saint Sara-la-Kali, he would have two hundred potions there, but the one we needed.

"Here." He pulled out a long vial with a shiny black liquid inside. "This is the one from the book."

"If you're sure, give it to him," Ryane said. "Now."

I kept sending Ramon my warmth while Theron adjusted his brother's head on his legs, tilted his chin up, and poured the thick liquid into Ramon's mouth.

On instinct, Ramon swallowed, then coughed, but he

didn't wake up. But we all saw it. In awe, we watched as Ramon's tremors lessened and the wounds in his arms healed.

"It worked," Theron whispered, his eyes bulged as if he couldn't believe what he was seeing. "I think it worked."

I finally pulled my hands away from Ramon. "It seems like it."

Ryane let out a long breath. "By Saint Sara-la-Kali ..." She checked his pulse. "His vitals are normal. I think he's just sleeping now."

"Help me," Theron said.

Ryane and I put our hands under Ramon's heavy body and helped Theron lay him back on the seat. Theron stayed by his side, seated on the floor, while Ryane scooted to the corner and kept on checking his vitals every couple of minutes.

And I took a spot in the backseat with Ellie.

She leaned into me. "That was scary," she whispered.

"To be honest, it still is," I whispered back. "We aren't one hundred percent sure what was in that potion."

She nodded. "True."

If the tension had been high inside the van before, now it was past the exploding point.

A couple of hours went by. Artan never stopped, not even when the others offered to take the wheel from him so he could get some rest. Some of us napped, others read, others just stared out, but no one spoke. The only noise inside the van was Ramon's loud breathing and the crunch of the snack bags as we ate the food we bought at the rest stop.

A new energy crackled through the air and sent a shudder up my arms.

Ramon jerked awake with a loud gasp.

With the sudden movement, Artan jerked the car again and my heart skipped a beat. Everyone was startled.

He sat up and glanced around, confused.

"Ramon," Theron called him. "You're fine. You're fine. We've got you."

"How ...?"

"How are you feeling?" Theron asked.

Ramon closed his eyes for a brief moment. "I don't know. I feel odd. Like I have a really bad hangover, but it's even worse than that." Ramon looked down his chest, his arms. "What happened?"

Theron tilted his head. "You don't remember?"

"Not much," Ramon said, his voice strained. "I remember running into the forest and distracting the alchemists, but then more came from the opposite direction. There were over twenty against me. There was nothing I could do." He paused as if trying to remember the rest. "Then ... then I was brought into a creepy house crawling with alchemists and strapped to a chair. After that, it's all a blur."

"After that, we came in and saved you," Theron explained.

"But ... what about my arms. I remember several IV needles in my arms. That has to have left some swelling and redness. I see nothing."

Theron ran a hand through his hair. His ponytail had come loose hours ago, and he hadn't redone it yet. "That ..."

"Guys," Artan called out.

"What?" Sloan asked, sounding annoyed.

I guess he felt like everyone else: apprehensive about Ramon's reaction to finding out he had been given a random potion his brother had stolen from the alchemists.

Perhaps it was a good thing Artan was interrupting them.

However, he surprised us all when he said, "We're here."

"WHAT?" CORA GOT UP FROM HER SEAT AND SCOOTED forward, closer to the driver's seat. "You mean at my enclave?"

"Yes," Artan answered. "We're almost there."

She looked side to side, as if trying to find recognizable markers of her home. She fisted the letter in her shaking hand, almost crumpling it. I wanted to hug her, to tell her everything would be okay. Even if we didn't find her family, she would be okay. She was okay. And we would always be here for her.

I made a mental note to do all that once we were out of the van. But once Artan parked at what looked like the entrance to the enclave, Cora practically trampled everyone as she jumped out of the van.

I watched as Rye shook his head. The frustration emanating from him was so strong, any tzigane could pick up on it without using enhanced abilities. Poor guy was probably trying to keep his hopes low until we found out if their families were alive.

"Watch out!" Artan shouted as the rest of us exited the van. "Get your weapons and be alert. Remember this most likely is a trap." He stared at me. "Stay behind us with Ellie."

I clenched my teeth, taking offense to his order. Did he think I couldn't protect myself? Or was he being considerate? Exhaling, I chose the latter.

Like an obedient saint, I stayed at the back with Ellie as the group approached the enclave's main road. My heart squeezed as I took in the damage. Dead and burned Golden Horehound, the shrub my mother had planted around our house during my childhood, surrounded the entrance. Beyond, what once had been white and beige houses were now gray and black. Their terracotta roofs were caved in, the windows broken and the doors missing. The wide stone path forming the streets were black and littered with debris.

Cora placed a hand over her mouth. "It's really destroyed."

Rye cupped her shoulder. "Maybe we should let the others check it out first. If they find something, they will let us know."

She rolled her shoulders, getting rid of his hand. "No! I have to see this for myself." She marched away, and Rye followed her.

"Stay together!" Artan called out. "Damn it."

"I'll go get them," Sloan said before following them.

I walked to Theron, who stared out to the burned enclave. "Was it like this when you two came check it out three years ago?"

He nodded. "There's more debris now. And the vegetation around the enclave was cared for." He pointed to the trees and shrubs outside the enclave's perimeter. "Now it's over-grown and dead."

"It looks worse now," Ramon said without hesitation. I had almost forgotten he had been with Theron when they rescued Cora, Rye, and Nico.

Suddenly, an image popped in my mind.

"Felix just showed me something," I said, turning to our left. The lion stepped out of the forest surrounding the enclave. He let out a low growl. "Here." I walked to him.

Artan followed me. "What is it?"

I gestured to a tall shrub. "Just behind there." I hadn't seen it yet, but I knew where it was from Felix's image.

Our friends approached while Artan pushed past the shrub. "A camp," he said.

I approached the makeshift camp. "Yes, but it seems to have been abandoned." The fire pit in the middle of the little camp was cold, and there were no tents, just the stakes that used to hold one, and a frayed rolled up mat tucked in under some raised tree roots, which had probably been forgotten.

"But ..." Ellie started, her eyes shining with curiosity. "That means someone was here, right? It means there were people, or tziganes around."

"Probably," Ryane said.

"But we don't know who yet." Artan crouched down as if he could have a better look from that height. "It could be other tziganes who were also lured here."

"Don't say that," I snapped. "We should hope this isn't a trap."

Artan stood and faced me. "I prefer believing the opposite. This is a trap until I'm proven wrong."

I held his stare, suddenly wanting to slap him to make him less stoic, less rude, less of an ass. He hadn't been like this before, and I hated that I couldn't help but hate him. Not just because of his lies, but because his attitude had taken a turn for the worse.

Deep down, I couldn't deny that I wanted to pull him to me, to hug him, to kiss him, to tell him I still liked him and I would always be here for him. Tell him that my feelings would never change even after he married Kizzy.

And yet, I hoped those feelings left me soon. It would be torture to love him while he took another woman to bed.

Ashamed of my thoughts and feelings, I spun around and marched back to the van.

Sloan ran toward us. "You guys. You have to see this."

Felix stayed behind while Theron, Ramon, Tomas, Ryane, Ellie, Artan, and I followed Sloan up a stone path, dodging debris and broken pavement, and turned into the main square on top of the hill.

Cora and Rye stood frozen beside the broken stone fountain, their eyes on the ground.

"What is it?" Artan asked, halting beside them.

I followed Cora's and Rye's gazes and gasped. "What is that?"

A big mark that looked like the footprint of a monster, with three long claws and one pointy heel, was pressed into the stone pavement. A couple of feet ahead, there was another one. Then another one. Then another one.

Theron examined the footprints. "What the hell is that?"

"What does this mean?" Ramon asked.

Cora turned wide, haunted eyes to us. "It means we're not alone."

12

WE DIVIDED INTO TWO GROUPS OF FOUR AND ONE GROUP OF three and patrolled the enclave, looking for whatever monster had left those footprints. But other than burned houses, broken doors and windows, and dead plants, we didn't find anything.

After almost two hours searching, we met back at the van. "What now?" Ryane asked.

I thought Cora would start yelling, but she surprised me. Her shoulders drooped; she remained a few steps back, visibly upset. I went to her and draped an arm over her shoulders. Perhaps now wasn't the time to tell her she would be fine and we were here for her, as it would only make her sadder, but I hoped my gesture was enough for now.

Artan looked up the sky. "The sun is setting. Since this day has been quite busy, I say we find a good spot in the forest and set up camp. We should rest and we'll look for survivors again tomorrow morning."

I was glad he hadn't mentioned anything about this entire thing being a trap. It would only irritate and upset Cora more. However, now that I thought about it, I wondered, was it really a trap? We had been here for hours and no alchemists had come out to attack us.

Unless they were waiting for nightfall ...

"Only if I can go out and buy something for us to eat," Tomas said.

"I'm with you," Theron said. "I don't want to have a snack or to have to kill a rabbit for dinner."

Ellie scrunched her nose. "Ew."

"All right," Artan said. "Tomas and Ryane can take the van and buy us dinner. Meanwhile, the rest of us set up camp."

Two hours later, we had four tents set up in a semi-circle, a nice fire burning in the center, and hot subs Tomas and Ryane had bought for us.

Once the sun had gone down, the temperature dropped, and even with the warrior's weather resistant uniform, it was too cold. We all sat around the fire eating, with thick coats or blankets over our shoulders.

"Just a reminder," I said between bites. "Please don't hurt the forest or Muma Padurii will take me away."

Ellie punched my shoulder. "Don't joke like that."

I made an "ow" with my mouth. "Her words, not mine!"

My best friend shuddered. "That woman gives me the creeps."

"With good reason," Theron said. "She's totally crazy."

Cora grabbed a small stick from the ground and played with it over the fire. "I had never seen her before."

"Be thankful for that," Artan muttered.

"Well, not that I saw much," Cora said. "She was behind all those vines."

Theron grunted. "She loves those vines."

"Yes, she does," I said, remembering how she had chased after us with those vines not even a month ago.

Time flew while we had fun. Or in my case, while I trained hard to become a real heart maiden. Until I found another heart flower and could follow its call, I would always have doubt.

But in the meantime, I pretended.

When Artan talked about a schedule for the night, I raised my hand. "I'll take first watch!"

"You should rest," he started.

"Everyone here knows I've been having problems sleeping. So, this way at least I'm doing something useful."

He frowned, but ended up agreeing.

Another hour passed while everyone finished eating, cleaned up, and retreated into their tents. Theron, Ramon, and Rye were in one, Sloan, Tomas, and Artan were in the second one, Cora and Ryane in the third one, and Ellie and I in the last one. Yawning, Felix sprawled near the dying fire and closed his eyes.

I picked up the dagger I had brought from Lovell's weaponry—I didn't know why I bothered carrying it. I would always go for magic first—and leaned against a thick tree in front of the tents. My plan was to walk the perimeter and send out my senses every ten minutes. That should be enough. Although, I was a bit worried about the big footprints we had found in the enclave. We hadn't seen them in the forest outside the enclave, and no one had any idea what it could be, but one thing we were sure of: There was something out there.

Hopefully, the big creature would stay away.

Artan retreated to his tent, but then he paused at the

entrance. He glanced my way. For some reason, I held his stare. My heart skipped a beat when he started toward me.

The orange light from the dying fire illuminated his profile, making his lines sharper. Stronger.

My head screamed for me to break the stare, but my heart cried that I couldn't.

He halted three feet from me. "Are you sure about this?"

I nodded. "Yes, I'm fine."

His brows curled down. "If you start feeling sleepy, call me. I'll take your place. Okay?"

"Okay," I whispered. His amber eyes fixed on mine; he didn't move. He didn't even blink. Why was he doing this to me? "You can go now," I said, my tone harsher than I had intended.

He let out a long breath. "Good night, Mirella."

I didn't say anything, but I couldn't stop from watching him as he marched to his tent and disappeared inside.

By Saint Sara-la-Kali, why was this so hard? Why couldn't I reign in my heart? Why did I still wish for what couldn't be mine? I tried telling myself that even if Artan wasn't engaged, I couldn't be with him. As the heart maiden, I couldn't have a partner. I always thought it was bullshit, but there were rules even I couldn't break.

Shaking my head, I started walking around the camp for my first patrol. I cast my senses out, hoping I could catch anything before they attacked us, but the forest was quiet. In this cold, there were no bugs, no animals out. It was just us and the plants—the ones that survived such harsh weather anyway.

I was almost completing the first loop when a dull pain started in the back of my skull.

No, not again.

Like before, the pain spread, bringing a vision with it.

Damara stood in front of me, smiling as I knelt to the ground in pain. "So pathetic." She flipped her long light brown hair over her shoulder as if she were a model posing for pictures. "And you call yourself a heart maiden? That's ridiculous."

"Shut up," I told her through gritted teeth.

She chuckled. "Prove to me you're the heart maiden. The one and only."

I glared at her. "Apparently, I'm not the one and only."

"Push through the pain. Push it away."

I pressed my fingers to my temples. "What? Are you trying to help me?"

"Well, the stronger you are, the more powers you have ... and the more powers I can steal from you later."

Fighting the pain, I stood. The pain ricocheted through my body, and I clenched my fists, holding it in. I wouldn't succumb in front of her. I couldn't.

"Go away."

"Only if you come with me."

"Damara, I know you're a hallucination."

She put her hands on her waist. "Are you sure about that?"

What did she mean? Of course she was a hallucination. I was having another one of those episodes. Just to prove I was right, the pain stabbed my chest hard and deep. I gasped. Soon, I would be on my knees again, and my friends would have to snap me out of it.

I glared at Damara. Couldn't I have hallucinations about someone else? "Go away," I repeated.

She lifted her arms to her sides, fire engulfing her hands.

"I'll hurt your friends. Then you'll know I'm not a hallucination." She threw the fire at the tents.

In a desperate attempt, I turned and extended my hand, calling her fire to me. It didn't work as well as I wanted. The fire fell on the ground instead of coming to my hand, but at least it hadn't reached the tents.

By Saint Sara-la-Kali, what was I saying? This was a hallucination. She couldn't really hurt them.

"It won't work," I told her. "I won't try to stop you anymore."

A wicked smile spread through her lips. "What if I tell you what the council is hiding from you?"

The pain drew holes in my skull, chest, and back. I pressed my hands to my temples, wishing that simple gesture could stop it. "This is *my* hallucination. Whatever you tell me, it'll be something I come up with. Just like in a dream."

"I expected better from you, Mirella." She tsked. "This is your *vision*, but you don't think as heart maidens that our minds are connected? When you have these visions, I see them too. I participate in them."

"W-what?" It couldn't be ... When I said that to the council, it had been a lie so they would let me come on this mission. Her mind wasn't really connected to mine. Or was it?

"I'm in here." She pushed her index finger into my forehead. The pain skyrocketed. "And you're in here." She touched her temple. "Now, follow me so I can tell you exactly what the council is hiding from you."

She spun around and walked past two thick trees.

I stared after her, trying to think about what to do. If this was a vision, I could follow her with no harm done. And if she was telling the truth, that she was really inside my head and would tell me what the elder council was hiding, then what did I have to lose?

I glanced at the camp, at the dying fire, the sleeping lion, and the four quiet tents. Just to be sure, I sent my senses out one more time. There was nothing out there.

Or this was all a hallucination, and I simply couldn't tell reality from the hallucinations.

Come on, I heard her voice inside my mind.

Crap, she really was in here.

A new wave of pain took over me, but I pushed past it and followed Damara into the forest.

Although the trees were leafless this time of the year, their branches were thick enough to hide most of the moonlight, making the path ahead hard to see. I raised my hand in front of me and conjured a small flame.

Damara was ten feet ahead. "Through here," she said without stopping.

Each step I took was a fight against the pain spreading through my body and the reasoning in my mind. Was this a really vision? If it were, it was different from the ones I had before. Was Damara really in my head? Did we have a connection? If we did, then I had to find a way to break it. I didn't want that crazy woman inside my head.

"Hurry up," I heard her voice, but didn't see her.

I went on, trailing after the sound of her voice and her steps crunching the dried leaves and fallen twigs.

The pain increased, pressuring my chest. It was getting harder to breathe. I fought it, but my vision blurred and my head swam with a wave of nausea.

I fell on my knees and my flame died. "D-Damara." She didn't answer. I tried looking around, but with my poor sight and the darkness of the forest, I couldn't see anything. I writhed in pain.

A man stepped out from the shadows, holding a branch burning at the tip. "Mirella," he said, his voice low.

I blinked, trying to see him.

Black clothes, black mask, shadow sword.

An alchemist.

Gasping, I scooted away. "Stay back!"

"Mirella, it's me."

I lifted my shaking hand. "Stay back or I'll kill you." A flame came to life in my palm. My aim would probably be off, but I could make my magic strong enough to stun him with a single hit.

The man crouched down, getting closer. "Mi ... it's me."

"I'm warning you!" I pulled my hand back to throw the flame at him. Letting go of the improvised torch, he lunged at me and caught my wrist before I could do anything. He held my arms to the side, and the flame died. "Let me go!"

I jerked back, but he grasped my shoulders tight and leaned into me. "Mirella, snap out of it." I knew this voice. He cupped my face and I froze. "It's Artan. I'm here."

"A-Artan?" I blinked fast, trying to clear my sight, but that only made my head hurt more. I closed my eyes and gritted my teeth.

Artan embraced her. "You're fine. I've got you. You'll be fine."

I sank into his arms, hurt and tired and confused. I took in deep breaths and focused on calming my mind and my heart. Slowly, my vision cleared and the pain retreated a little. I was still confused about before, but I knew this—Artan hugging me—wasn't a hallucination.

"What happened?" I croaked.

"I was about to ask you that," he whispered in my ear. "I woke up and decided to check on you, but I couldn't find you."

I pulled back and looked around. We really were away from our camp. "I was patrolling the perimeter when the pain started. Then Damara showed up. She said she wasn't a hallucination. That we are connected and she can really get inside my head."

Artan's brows curled down. "What else did she say?"

"She taunted me about whatever secret the elder council is keeping from me. She said that if I followed her, she would tell me." I swallowed, realizing now how stupid I had been. "I don't know why I followed her. Maybe because I thought I was dreaming? I don't know. But I followed her." I opened my arms, gesturing to the forest. "And here we are."

He brushed a curl from my face. "You're fine now. I've got you."

"I'm sorry."

"For?"

"For leaving my post. For not being able to control whatever is happening to me and losing it completely."

He cupped my face again, his gaze locked on mine. Only a sliver of light came from the burning branch he was holding beside us, but it was enough to show me the emotion shining in his eyes. "Whatever it is, we'll figure it out. Together."

"Artan ..." I started scooting back, but he grasped my arm with his other hand and kept me in place.

"No, don't run away." He sighed. "I mean it, Mirella. I'll always protect you, no matter what."

His words ... his stare ... his beautiful face ... his strong body ...

I was powerless. Every reason why not to love him flew

out the window—in that moment, I couldn't remember a single one—and I knew, I knew I was a goner.

His eyes flicked to my lips and he leaned into me.

A scream echoed through the forest.

Alert, Artan and I jumped apart.

"What was that?" I asked, calling a ball of fire in my hands. Light inundated the area, but all I saw were trees.

"I don't know." His feet were spread wide, and his hands poised at his sides, ready to strike.

Another scream filled the air.

My stomach dropped. "I think it's coming from our camp."

Artan took off and I ran alongside him. When we reached camp, we found the group standing together beside the now dead fire.

"What's going on?" Artan asked, approaching the group.

A new scream rang out—deep and guttural. The hairs on the back of my neck rose.

Ellie glanced at us. "He's in pain, but we don't know what to do."

"Who?" I asked, stepping closer.

In front of the group, Theron was knelt beside a trembling Ramon.

"I already tried healing him, but it's not working," Ryane said. "His heartbeat is through the roof. I don't know how to bring it down."

The warmth of my fire had helped before. Perhaps I could make him a little better for a moment, so we could figure out what was going on. I knelt beside Theron and reached for Ramon.

The moment I touched him, he jerked and spread his long body on the ground. He opened his eyes and let out another scream. Gasping, I fell back on my butt. Everyone retreated.

Ramon's eyes were red, his teeth were sharp like fangs, and his scream ... it was more like a deep growl.

He started convulsing again. His limbs extended. His bones cracked. His clothes ripped away. The hair on his body grew and spread.

A moment later, he lifted his head and growled at us.

Ramon had become a werewolf.

13

WE WERE ALL SO STUNNED, NOBODY MOVED OR EVEN THOUGHT about moving. Not until Ramon let out another growl and lunged at us with his powerful wolf legs.

We scampered around the camp, while Ramon chased after us.

"What do we do?" Cora asked, raising her hands in front of her. I wasn't sure punching a werewolf would be the best option, but I knew her sword was inside the tent. She wouldn't use it even if she had it with her.

"Don't hurt him!" Theron shouted. "Remember, it's Ramon!"

Shit. How could we contain him without hurting him? He was a freaking werewolf!

Felix jumped into the fray and engaged Ramon. They circled each other, giving us some breathing room while we thought of a plan.

Don't hurt him, I told Felix.

Busy with his blood-lusting opponent, the lion didn't answer me.

"Any ideas how to contain a *ruv*?" Rye asked.

"A what?" I asked, confused.

"It means wolf," Theron snapped. "Or werewolf."

By Saint Sara-la-Kali, how much crazier could my world get? Tziganes, alchemists, revenants, forest protectors, wyverns ... and now *ruvs*, or werewolves. Soon I would be meeting centaurs and mermaids.

"We need to calm him down," Artan said.

Ryane reached inside a leather satchel. "I don't have any elixir for that."

"What about the potions we got from the alchemists?" Sloan asked.

Tomas gestured to the wolf a few feet from us. "Wasn't that what made him like this in the first place? I say we stay away from those for now."

"We don't know what made him like this," Theron said. "But you're right. We shouldn't test any more of those potions."

"We need to stun him somehow," I said, trying to think if any of our magic could do something like that.

"Stun!" Theron eyes widened. "I should have some tranquilizer we use on heart animals in my pack." He scurried inside his tent. Ten seconds later, he had a tranquilizer gun and dart.

"Isn't that too strong?" Artan asked.

Theron put the dart into the gun. "It is, but isn't he strong now too?"

"Good point."

Theron took a step closer and pointed the gun toward the big, brown wolf fighting the big, white lion. It was a sight to see. The moment he pulled the safety off, Ramon snapped his head to his brother. He bared his teeth.

"Shit," Theron muttered.

Ramon lunged at him. Artan raised his hand and sent a blast of wind out. Theron squeezed the trigger. The dart buried itself in Ramon's chest, and he fell on the ground with a loud thump.

Ramon trembled for a moment, fighting against the drug, but soon, his body started changing. His limbs shrank; the hair over his body disappeared. Theron grabbed a throw blanket from inside the tent and rushed to his brother.

"Hey," he said, covering Ramon's naked body with the blanket.

Ramon trembled. "That was real, right?" his voice was low and raspy. "I just became a werewolf, right?"

"Yes, you did."

Clutching the blanket, Ramon sat up. He hissed and placed a hand on his head. "Everything hurts." He looked up at his brother and then at us. "How ... how did that happen?"

Rye stepped closer. "We aren't sure."

"I'm sorry." Ramon exhaled deeply. "I can't believe I attacked you all."

"It seemed you weren't in control," Cora said. "So you're forgiven."

"Don't worry about that now," I told him.

He glanced my way, then averted his eyes.

"We need to find a way to control the change," Artan said. "We can't have you involuntarily transforming on us."

His eyes hard, Ramon stood. "Then try to find how to get rid of this, because I didn't sign up to become a freaking *ruv*." He glared at Theron. "It was that damn potion you gave me."

"We don't know that!" Theron retorted. "The alchemists could have done something to you when they kidnapped you."

"Why would the alchemists turn me into a *ruv*?"

The bickering continued, but I didn't pay attention. A dark cloud brushed against me, and I turned my back on the group, watching the forest. There was something out there ... someone.

"An alchemist," I whispered.

The group went silence.

Movement behind a tree caught our attention.

"He's getting away!" Artan shouted.

We ran after the alchemist. Felix was much faster than all of us and in ten seconds, jumped on the alchemist, making him fall face-first on the forest floor.

Artan and Theron got him and escorted him back to our camp. In the moonlight, we recognized the red mask he was wearing.

"You better start talking," Artan said, tying his hands behind his back.

The alchemist laughed. "Ah, don't spoil it. It has been fun to watch you."

Artan tightened the ropes, until it was biting into the alchemist's skin. "Don't make me torture you for an answer."

I frowned, not liking how cold Artan could get. Not even an hour ago he had been embracing and comforting me, and now he was acting like a thug.

Ramon came out from his tent, wearing a new warrior's uniform. Thankfully, we all had more than one. He marched to the alchemist and pressed his sword to the man's neck. "What did you do to me?"

Another laugh bubbled out of the alchemist's mouth. "We didn't do anything. You did it yourself."

"What do you mean?"

"This is too much fun to keep to myself," the alchemist

said. If it weren't for the red mask covering the lower half of his face, I would say he was smiling. "You've stolen potions from us. I'm assuming you took one of them."

Theron paled. "You mean you had a potion to transform a person into a *ruv*?"

"Well, to be honest, we turned him into a werewolf before, while we were experimenting with him." He chuckled. "The potion you took was probably a bland one. A potion that didn't work and we still had it to study it." He stopped laughing. "Shame you didn't steal a more powerful one from our large stock of unusual potions."

"How do I reverse this?" Ramon asked through gritted teeth.

"You can't," the alchemist answered. "Once you're a werewolf, you can't reverse it. Even if you live to be a hundred years old, you're dying as a werewolf."

Ramon groaned. "You just said you have unusual potions of every kind. You must have an antidote."

"Our direct experiments are so good, you can't undo it. You're now a real werewolf, as if you had been born one or bitten."

Wow, that was incredible in a creepy way.

Artan loomed over the alchemists. "What kind of alchemist are you?"

Since we had first bumped into them this morning, they looked and felt different from the alchemists we usually fought.

"Wouldn't you like to know?"

"Are you the ones who lured us here?" Theron stepped closer. A third strong warrior pressing against the enemy. It seemed a little excessive. "Why?"

The alchemist frowned. "Lured you here? No. I've been just following you since you left the manor this morning."

Cora looked at me and I shrugged. What did it mean? We were dealing with two groups of alchemists?

"Why are you following us?" Ramon asked.

The alchemist tilted his head, grazing his neck on the tip of Ramon's sword. He glanced over Ramon's shoulder and his eyes met mine. "You have the heart maiden. Every alchemist in the world wants the heart maiden."

Artan groaned. He punched the alchemist. The alchemist fell on his knees. "You're never having her," Artan spat.

The alchemists laughed again, a chilling sound that send a shudder down my spine. "Don't be so certain of that."

All of a sudden, he rolled his eyes to the back of his head, and all we could see was white. His body started shaking violently. And then he jerked free of the ropes tying his hands as if they had been made of cotton candy. He grabbed the blade of Ramon's sword with both hands and drove it into his chest.

The alchemist killed himself.

14

ARTAN STRAPPED HIS SWORD TO HIS BELT AND LOOKED AROUND. "Everyone ready?"

Some of us mumbled a yes, while others nodded. I didn't say anything as I finished tying my boots up.

It had been a long night, and for someone who rarely slept, that was saying something.

After the alchemist killed himself, we all had been so stunned that it took us a moment to move. Artan and Theron went into the forest to dispose of the body, while the rest of us went back to sleep. Or tried to. If I was feeling confused and had too much to think about, I was sure the others, especially Ramon felt the same.

My mind reeled with the thought of another kind of alchemists out there. What did that mean? What did they want? Did we fight them the same way? There were so many questions about that matter.

And now there was the matter of Ramon's lycanthropy. Artan was right; we couldn't have him transforming into a werewolf on us without warning. But how did we contain it?

Or, like Ramon had said, how did we reverse it? The alchemist had said there was no way to reverse it, but I doubted it.

In the end, I slept for less than two hours before I was awoken by the sound of shuffling outside. When I exited my tent, I found Artan, Theron, Sloan, Rye, and Cora already having breakfast. Someone had gone to buy food for us at the nearest town, and now there were paper bags on a blanket beside the cold fire.

After waking up Ellie and eating, I packed and left to get everything ready. We didn't know what would happen now, if we were finally going to meet Cora's family or be caught by alchemists, but we wanted to have everything ready in case we needed to flee.

Ramon was the last one to roll out of bed, and he seemed in a worse mood than usual.

"I'm ready," Cora answered Artan, sounding excited.

By Saint Sara-la-Kali, I prayed this wasn't a trap and that we really found her family here. And Rye's and Nico's family too. And maybe the entire enclave.

But, Artan had been right. If everyone was alive, why hadn't they contacted Bellville before now? They didn't need to wait three years for that.

My heart longed for them, but my head told me it was futile to hope for impossible things.

Wearing our uniforms and with our weapons at our waists, we set out to explore the enclave. This time, we didn't separate. Artan hadn't said the words out loud, but I knew why: We would be better off fighting together, than alone.

We explored inch by inch, turning over fallen debris, going through the ruins of every house and building, even when they seemed like they would crumble on top of our heads at any moment. We found lots of personal objects: books, picture frames, clothes ... but all burned to a crisp. If the tziganes were alive, they had fled with nothing.

Rye stopped in front of the next house we were about to explore. "This was Nico's house."

My heart tugged. It hurt to walk through the house and see where he had lived, eaten, and slept with his family. I tried not paying much attention to the personal objects, because I was sure to cry.

Like Cora was crying. She tried to contain the tears, but she couldn't. She swallowed each sob, though, and cried in silence. How she didn't break down and curl into a ball and rock like a baby, I didn't know. If it were me, I would probably have fainted a couple of times.

We went through a couple more houses, then Rye froze in front of another one.

"This was his house," Cora said.

This time, Cora and Rye stayed outside. She hugged him and he held on to her, burying his face in her neck.

My eyes filled with tears.

Shit, we would find Cora's house at one point, and I wasn't sure I was ready for her reaction. Or mine.

We kept going for hours.

Finally, we reached the main square on top of the hill. There was only a few more streets on the other side. Which meant, we hadn't found anything yet. No tzigane, no trap.

What the hell was this, then? Why had Cora been called here?

"Let's take a break," Artan said.

At once, Ryane spread a blanket on the hard stone pavement, and Ellie brought out snacks from her pack. They sat down and called us to join them. The guys stood around them, eating a couple of chips and drinking water.

Cora walked around the square, too unsettled to stop.

I felt the same, so instead of taking a break, I kept exploring. Like in Lovell, this enclave's administration buildings were around the square. I had easily identified the infirmary and the school. I went through them, and other than the objects that had been left behind, I found nothing. I even went through the few intact cabinets in the infirmary, hoping I could magically find a potion that would help Ramon. But no such luck. Other than broken vials of antiseptics and antibiotics, and potions for pain and other health issues, there were no special elixirs here.

After, I moved to the main building. I paused a few feet from the entrance and looked up. The building had been three stories before, but now it was barely one in some parts. I wondered if I threw a pebble at the right place, if the rest of the building would come down.

And I was about to enter it.

Bracing myself, I pushed open the broken front door. It came off its hinges. I jumped back before if fell on my feet, and I scrunched my nose at the loud thump that echoed when it hit the ground.

Stepping over it, I walked through the doorway. The sound of something crackling and a string pulling made me stop. What was that?

Then *woosh*.

The string let go and out from the dark end of the room, dozens of arrows flew toward me.

My heart stopped.

Something crashed into me and pushed me down. My back hit the floor and pain irradiated down my spine. Shit.

Ramon pushed up from over me. "Are you all right?"

I looked around, confused. The arrows had flown toward me; Ramon somehow miraculously showed up and pushed me out of the way. I stared at the dozen arrows embedded in the wall. If he hadn't known, if he hadn't pushed me down, right now I would be ...

Theron burst into the room. "What happened?"

Artan was right behind him. "Where did these arrows come from?"

Ramon stood. I only noticed my hands were shaking when he offered me his and I took it. "I think it was a booby trap," Ramon said, pulling me up. "Unless it's something else."

"Those weren't there before," Cora said from the doorway.

"Yeah, we would have known," Rye said from behind her.

"Then I can only guess it was put there by alchemists," Artan said.

"Which means calling us here was really a trap," Theron said.

"We're not sure of that yet," Cora snapped. "Other than the one alchemist, no one else is around."

Artan stepped closer to me. He eyed me from head to toe and back. "Are you okay?"

I stared at Ramon. "H-how did you know?"

He pointed to his ears. "I guess having enhanced were-wolf hearing comes in handy."

But he had saved me. I had never guessed Ramon of all people would save me. "I thought you hated me."

"I'm just a grump. I don't hate you or anyone." Ramon paused. "Besides ..."

"What?"

"He asked me not to say anything yet," Ramon grumbled.

"What are you talking about?" I asked.

He glanced at Theron, then back at me. "You know what? You two should know. I'm tired of keeping secrets."

Theron took a step closer. "What?"

Ramon swallowed hard. "Mirella, you're our sister."

15

———

WAS HE JOKING RIGHT NOW? "WHAT?"

Theron took a step back. "What did you say?"

Ramon let out a long sigh. "My *dat* is your *dat*," he said. I fought the urge to rub my ears, because I couldn't be hearing him right.

"What ...?" Theron pulled at his long hair. "Explain what you're saying."

"There have been little clues," Ramon said. "I've noticed how *dat* looks at Mirella, and I also saw him speaking with Risa twice. They looked like they were arguing, but they were sort of hidden, as if they didn't want anyone to see them together."

"So you assumed Mirella is our *phen*?" Theron asked, his tone hard.

I was more confused by the second. "Ph-what?"

"*Phen*," Ramon said. "Means sister. And *phal* is brother." He turned his dark eyes to Theron. "To answer your question, no, I didn't assume anything. I cornered *dat* and asked him what was going on. And he admitted that he loved Risa, always had, and that Mirella was his *chey*." He looked at me. "Although, he didn't know it until recently."

"That," I whispered. My head spun. "That doesn't make sense."

"He told me," Ramon continued. "He and Risa met when they were teenagers. They had been engaged to other people already, but they didn't love their fiancés. They loved each other. But they didn't surrender to their love. Not until a few years later, after our *daj* died." If I wasn't mistaken, their mother had died when Theron was only a couple of months old. "Risa hadn't been married yet, and they ended up having an affair. Risa got pregnant, but when he asked her about it, she told him it was from a *gadjo*. She pushed him away, and then Risa was banished from Lovell and disappeared."

"So, Mirella is the daughter of a *gadjo*, not our *dat*," Theron said. The hard edge of his words made me even more uncomfortable than I already felt.

"No," Ramon said. "Our father confronted Risa about it and Risa confessed. She lied to protect our *dat*. She knew Lovell would banish her and somehow find a way of punishing him for what they had done, so she lied."

I shook my head. "That doesn't make sense."

"He wants to tell you, but for some reason, your mother doesn't want you to know." Ramon paused. "You're our sister, Mirella."

I took a step back and bumped into the blunt end of a couple of arrows. I jumped to the side, my heartbeat skyrocketing. "No ..."

Ramon tilted his head. "Is it so bad to be our *phen*?"

That wasn't the problem. I mean, I didn't know how to feel about that right now, but I would deal with that later. The problem was finding out I had been lied to—again.

I was always being lied to.

Would the lies ever end?

I snorted. Who was I to complain about lies? I was always lying too. Lies swam all around me, and I was so sick and tired of them.

"Excuse me," I muttered, pushing past my friends.

Artan grabbed my wrist, making me stop. "Mirella ..."

I tugged at my arm. "Let me go."

He must have noticed the bite in my words, because he eased his grip and released me. I marched out of the building.

"Where are you going?" Ellie asked. She had been outside, along with Sloan, Tomas, and Felix. They must have heard everything. They knew everything. When I didn't answer, she rushed after me. "Hey, talk to me."

"I'm going to the van," I barked out without slowing down. "I need some time alone."

Ellie winced as if I had slapped her, but she didn't push it. She also let me go.

Once I turned the corner to the next street and was out of sight, I ran.

An hour after I stomped away from the group, I felt a little better, if not silly. When Ramon revealed the truth, I had been mad, but not mad at him or my friends. And yet, my actions probably said otherwise.

Although I was calmer now, my mind still reeled.

I paced around the van, thinking about it all for the thousandth time. Dolan was my father. Sheila was my grandmother—shit, and to think how many times I had wished that was true? And Theron and Ramon were my half-brothers. I was indeed one hundred percent tzigane and exactly half Lovell and half Bellville.

I kicked a small rock and sighed. My mother had lied to me again. I thought we had been past the lies. I thought that finally she and I were starting to have a good, truthful relationship. I guess I was wrong.

I wondered if she had been truthful about anything during my life. Probably not. Probably every word that came out of her mouth was laced with lies.

Lies. Lies. Lies.

I hated lies.

By Saint Sara-la-Kali. I had a father. And two brothers.

Ramon and Theron.

Theron. My friend, Theron. My brother, Theron. Now I understood why we had a telepathic connection. But why didn't I have one with Ramon? Well, not even Theron had one, not as strong as ours, at least. Perhaps Ramon was so closed overall, he was closed in his mind, too.

I frowned, wondering how Theron was feeling about me now. He had been as shocked as me ... as mad as me. But my anger had passed, most of it anyway. Had his?

The sun was starting its descent when I heard their footsteps approaching.

I stiffened, waiting.

From the distance, I saw Artan, Ryane, Tomas, Sloan, Ellie, Theron, Ramon, and Felix.

I frowned. "Where's Cora and Rye?"

"She wanted to stay and search some more," Sloan said, walking up to me.

Ryane halted by our side. "Even though I'm pretty sure we went through the entire enclave."

"She needs closure, I guess," Tomas added.

I glanced up at the sky. "But it's getting dark." And it would be colder too.

"Yeah, I told them to come back before it gets dark," Artan said, joining us. "I don't want them to run into any booby traps."

I gasped. "Were there more?"

He nodded. "Yes. A lot more."

What did that mean? That the alchemists rigged the place to catch us? So it was a trap? If it was, why hadn't they shown up yet?

Ellie appeared by my side. "How are you feeling?"

"Confused," I confessed. "But I'm okay." I glanced at Theron and Ramon. My brothers. Standing a few feet behind the group, Ramon nodded his chin once at me, but Theron didn't look my way. In fact, he marched to the other side of the van, where I couldn't see him.

My heart sank.

Was he really treating me like I was a criminal now?

"He'll come around," she said in a low voice.

I sighed. "Will he?"

"This was a big shock to you guys. He's confused now and doesn't know how to feel or act right now."

I cocked my eyebrows at her. "What about me? I'm like that too, but I'm not glaring at him as if I could punch him if he gets too close."

Ellie rolled her eyes. "Men. So overly dramatic."

I almost laughed. Almost. It had too much going on inside me, the laughter got lost in there.

We wouldn't solve our feelings today. Maybe not even this week. Or this month. It was better to let it go for now and focus on the mission.

Easier said than done.

Forcing myself to focus, I cleared my throat. "So, what's the plan?"

"We make camp and continue looking tomorrow," Artan said.

"There's nothing else to look for," Sloan said in a low voice.

"I know," Artan said. "But the other option is simply to pick up our things and go home."

"I don't think Cora is ready," Ryane said.

"I know, but we can't stay here forever." Artan reached for the van's door right beside me. "I'll give her one more day, then we need to go back. Being out in the open is too risky."

Sloan nodded. "I still think it's a trap."

"All we can do is stay alert and fight if the alchemists come." Artan opened the door and picked up the nearest bag. "All right. Let's go back to our campsite from last night." He passed the bags around, calling our names. Theron, Ramon, Sloan, Tomas, Ryane, and Ellie. They got their bags then stepped out, ready to march into the forest beyond. "Here's yours." Eyes locked on mine, Artan handed me my bag. "How are you?"

I frowned, realizing he had left my bag for last on purpose. "You heard Ellie and me. I'm fine."

"Mirella." He reached for me. Like a stupid, lovesick girl, I let him cradle my hand in his. "I'm here. For anything. If you want to talk, if you want to cry, even if you want a punching bag. I can be that, too."

My breath caught. My chest constricted.

Why, oh why did he had to be so sweet sometimes?

I wanted to hate him. Because honestly, that was the only way I would get over him.

Gently, I pulled my hand away. "Thank you."

I turned away from him and joined the rest of the group. Except for Theron. He was off to the side, a few feet from all of us.

I knew he needed some time, but this was ridiculous. He couldn't treat me like this. I wasn't at fault here. If he wanted to blame someone, then it had to be his father and my mother. I was innocent on all accounts.

The feeling built up inside me, and in matter of seconds, I felt like I was about to explode. I had to let it all out. It might be the wrong time, but he would hear me out.

I spun around and opened my mouth to yell at him.

"Guys!" Cora's shout made me swallow the angry words that had been at the tip of my tongue. "Guys!"

We all turned toward the enclave's main entrance. Waving her hand high, Cora ran to us, Rye following a few steps behind.

"She's holding something," Ryane said.

Ellie narrowed her eyes. "What is that?"

Smiling wide, Cora skidded to a stop in front of us. "I've found something."

16

"I just found this." Cora showed us the leather-bound book in her hands. "It's a journal. My father's journal, where he wrote in code and left messages for me."

"That's ..." Artan pressed his lips tight, before continuing. "Where did you find this?"

"At my house," she said, her voice eager.

"I thought we had already searched your house," Sloan said.

"We went back," Rye explained. "She wanted to. But then we found that."

"How did we miss it the first time?" Artan asked. His voice and the hardness in his eyes didn't hide his suspicion.

"It was behind a false wall," Cora said. "I remembered to look for it when we went back." Her smile widened. "Here it is! Proof that they are still alive."

"I don't understand," Ramon said. It was his first words since he had come from the enclave earlier. "Why is this proof? It could have been there for the last three years."

Cora's eyes sparkled. "There's a message inside." She

opened the book at the first page. "It's in code, and I already translated half of it, but apparently, my father left the journal so I could find it, and now I can use it to find him."

That sounded so …

"It's crazy," Artan said.

"It's too convenient," Sloan said.

"I smell a trap," Theron barked.

They all read my mind.

Cora gripped the book tight. "Please, believe me. I know his handwriting. I know the code. It's my father and he wants me to find him. I can't ignore this."

Felix turned to Cora and sniffed the book.

He sent an image to my mind. A trail.

"I think …" I started, trying to decipher his message. "I think Felix can follow the scent of the book."

Cora's eyes widened. "He can?" Felix nodded his big head. Cora bounced on her feet. "Show us the way, Felix."

I frowned, once more intrigued by her behavior. She had been too eager, too chipper since she got the first letter. So different from the stoic and quiet warrior she usually was. But, who was I to say anything? I had known her for only a few months. Perhaps she had always been like this and I didn't know any different.

Felix sent an image inside my mind: Artan standing beside me.

I looked at Artan. "He wants to know if he can take us there."

Artan stuffed his chest. "Well, at least the lion respects my position as team leader."

I fought not to roll my eyes at him.

Ellie took my arm and leaned into me. "Do you remember the last time we followed the lion?"

"He was under Damara's spell then," I said, defending Felix.

"What if he is under a spell right now?" Sloan asked.

I channeled my power and sent my senses into Felix's mind—it was always open to me. I searched for a threat in every corner of his mind and found nothing wrong. "He's fine. No one is controlling him right now." I turned my gaze to Artan. "So?"

Artan looked up at the darkening sky. "It's going to be night soon."

"We have flashlights," Rye said.

"I can help too." I turned my palm up and conjured a bright flame. No heat, but pure light.

Artan looked at each one of us. Finally, he glanced to Cora, then Felix. "All right. Lead the way, Felix."

After grabbing our weapons, we threw our bags inside the van again and followed Felix into the forest.

Felix and Cora took the front. Rye was right behind them. Then Artan and me, Sloan, Tomas and Ryane, Ramon and Ellie, and several feet back, Theron tagged along.

The first ten minutes we hiked through the forest were in silence. Then soft chatter started from each group.

I glanced at Artan. "Do you still think this is a trap?"

He shrugged. "I don't know. Sometimes I'm certain it is, but then, other than the booby traps, which could have been installed several years ago, no alchemists have attacked us directly, and now this ..." He gestured to Cora in front of the group.

"I know." I let out a long breath. "It's hard to argue with that."

"I know I sound skeptical all the time. It's probably the warrior in me, but I honestly hope we find her family."

My heart tugged, then melted in a puddle inside my chest.

Again, I wondered why it wasn't easier to hate him. Couldn't he be mean all the time? This hot and cold, pull and push thing was making me dizzy. He was getting married, for goodness sake. He had to let me go.

If he wouldn't do it, then I had to be the one to put distance between us.

I halted. "Hm, I … I need to talk to Ellie about something."

Artan's eyes bugged for a moment, but he nodded once and kept on moving forward. I stayed in place until I reached Ellie and Ramon. Then, I started walking with them.

"Is he still bugging you?" Ellie asked. Her voice was low, but with his wolf hearing, I was sure Ramon had heard her.

"A little," I confessed.

"So, I wasn't wrong that there was something going on between you and Artan," Ramon said, surprising me.

I tilted my head. "You're very perceptive."

Ramon shrugged. "I'm quiet, not blind. Besides, when people think you're ignoring them, they show you their true colors. I see much more because people think I don't care."

I had never thought about that, but I guess it made sense.

I looked at my hands. "Aren't you upset at me, too?"

He narrowed his eyes at me. "Why? It's not your fault. To be honest, I don't think there's anyone to blame here. At first, I was upset with my *dat* for keeping it from us, then a little upset with your *daj* for not letting him tell us, but I guess she must have had her reasons." He paused. "I'm sorry I just blurted it out. I should have let her tell you."

I shook my head. "She wouldn't have told me. I would have lived the rest of my life without knowing it." So many times I had felt jealous of the little girls in my dance classes whose fathers came to pick them up, or dropped everything to watch their recitals. I had never had that. But now I had a father. By Saint Sara-la-Kali, I had a father. "I still have to get used to this truth, but I'm glad you told me."

One corner of his lips curled up. "Me too."

I almost tripped on my own feet. Ramon was smiling? Sort of? That was new and unexpected.

An image appeared in my mind. A small clearing of dirt packed ground and a rocky hill right behind it.

Felix was letting me know we had arrived.

"I think we're here," I said.

We rushed forward, joining the others past the trees, and into the clearing. Darkness was falling fast and the moon's shine was still too weak. I raised my hand, conjuring my flame and inundating the clearing with warm orange light.

Cora looked around. "I don't see anything. Anyone." She turned to Felix. "What is this place?"

With a low growl, Felix walked to the base of the rocky hill. Pointing our flashlights and my flame forward, we followed him.

Cora gasped as we took in what was spread over the rocks. Burned books, clothes and shoes, toys, blankets, and even small furniture like side tables and stools.

"What is this?" Rye asked.

Artan crouched down beside the objects. "I'm not sure."

Cora picked up another book from the pile, similar to the other she was holding. A tear slid down her face as she flipped through it. "Another one of my father's journal."

From the other side of the group, Theron asked, "But what does this mean?"

"I don't know," Rye said, his voice low.

Another tear escaped Cora's eyes. "It can't be." She threw both books into the pile. "It can't end here. There has to be another trail. There has to be more." She glanced around. "We have to find them. They are out there. I'm sure they are out there."

Rye stepped right into her and gripped her shoulders. "Cora, calm down."

She pushed him away. "Calm down?" Her voice rose. "I have lived in mourning for the last three years. Suddenly, I receive a sliver of hope and start dreaming my family has come back to me." A sob cut past her throat. "I'm not going to calm down. I won't calm down! Not until I find them!"

"Cora ..." Rye reached for her again.

She slapped his hands away. "Leave me alone!"

All of a sudden, the ground shook underneath our feet. Ellie grabbed my arm in an effort to steady herself, but we almost went down together. Ryane fell on her ass, and Cora bumped into the rocks.

"What's going on?" Artan asked.

The shaking increased as a loud noise started.

A loud roar came from somewhere behind the rocks.

Then, from an almost imperceptible opening hidden among the rocks forming the hill, our enemy stepped out.

17

Ellie paled. "Is that ...?"

I gasped. "It can't be."

Artan pulled out his sword from the scabbard at his waist. "It's a dragon."

The huge creature exited the cave, each step shaking the ground and bringing down little rocks from the hill. Its scaly brown-gray skin looked thick and slimy. His legs were the size of the trees around us. Its paws ... that was where the footprints the enclave were from. This dragon had been raiding the enclave.

The dragon halted and lowered his head a little. Its brown and yellow snake-like eyes blinked once, twice, then he opened his huge mouth, revealing too many rows of sharp fangs, and let out a hair-raising roar.

My stomach dropped as we scooted back.

"This is worse than the wyverns," Ellie said, her voice trembling. She was right. This dragon was probably the size of the three wyverns put together, and it looked much tougher.

Felix let out a growl and raced around the dragon, distracting him. I reached for him and sensed his fear and adrenaline as he taunted the dragon so he wouldn't attack us.

"What do we do?" I asked. "Fight?"

"It'll be hard to fight it," Artan said. "Our magic doesn't do much against it because of its thick skin."

"Not even my fire?" I asked, remembering the wyverns had fled when I threw my fire at them.

"It can breathe fire," Sloan said.

Artan nodded. "Yeah, it's immune to fire."

"How can we kill it, then?" Ellie squeaked. Once more I was proud of her. As the only human in the group, she should hiding behind our legs. I was sure she wanted to, but she held on.

"We can't," Ramon said, stepping up to the front of the group. "We have to distract it, then get away."

"And how do you suggest we do that?" Ryane asked.

Just then, the dragon turned around and its spiky tail swiped at us. We jumped back as the tail swooshed past us.

Ramon took off the top part of his uniform. "I'm going to wolf out and help Felix. We'll lead the dragon away from here, in the opposite direction. Meanwhile, you all get away."

"Are you crazy?" I asked. Because he had to be. "You just did that with the alchemists back at the gas station and look how great that turned out."

Theron stood beside Ramon. "She's right. Don't do it."

"Besides, last time you were a *ruv*, you tried to attack us," Tomas said. "How do you think you'll control it now?"

"I'll find a way." Ramon grinned at Artan. "I'm not the team leader. Sorry, Artan, but this is *my* order."

He didn't wait for an answer. Ramon turned into a wolf, ripping his pants into little pieces, and ran toward the dragon.

My heart stopped. "Ramon!"

Artan caught my arm. "He's gone. We can't argue about it anymore. We need to act. Let's go."

He tugged me along, and the others followed us. Theron was the last one to come. We ran back and huddled beside the van.

"What are we going to do now?" Ryane asked.

Sloan sighed. "I don't know. Everything is kind of messed up."

Artan nodded. "We still don't know if the letter was a trap or the real thing, and we keep getting derailed by other matters."

"Like ... a dragon," Ellie whispered, her blue eyes bugged.

"You've seen Muma Padurii and wyverns, and you're shocked about a dragon?" Rye asked.

"Well, did you see the size of that thing?" Ellie asked. "I thought it was going to eat us alive."

"It was," Theron snapped. "If it wasn't for Ramon, we would be all dead right now."

"That was a brave thing for him to do," Ryane said.

"A lot of brave, but also stupid," Tomas said.

"Yeah, dragons are strong creatures." Sloan tsked. "I hope that between Ramon and Felix, they distracted the dragon and got away fine."

Theron clenched his fists. "This is crazy. I'm going after him."

Cora shook her head. "No, Theron. Give him more time. He's just—"

Theron put his finger in Cora's face. "This is all your fault. We're in this mess because of you." She froze, in shock.

"Theron," I rasped without meaning to.

He glared at me. "You too. This is your fault, too. If you

hadn't lied to the elder council about this mission, they wouldn't have let you come and we wouldn't be in this mess. And Ramon wouldn't be running from a dragon right now."

I gasped at the rage in his expression and his words.

"Hey, man," Rye said, stepping closer to Cora. "You're being harsh."

Theron turned his hard eyes to Rye. "Stay out of this."

Rye stood tall, clearly not afraid of Theron. "This is about my family, too."

"Wake up, you idiots," Theron said. "Your families are dead."

Hand over her mouth, Cora gasped and Rye hissed.

My heart squeezed in pain. I didn't like seeing my friends arguing, but I had no idea what to do to make them stop. It seemed that if I tried saying or doing anything, Theron would turn on me again, and I wasn't sure I could handle that.

"Theron!" Artan called out. "This is not the time to argue."

Theron stepped up to Artan. "You ... you stay out of this. You're just here out of duty. You don't care about us, you don't like Bellville, and you barely knew about Cora and Rye until a couple of months ago."

All right, I couldn't stay out of that.

"Theron," I started, but the rest of my speech was lost as pain exploded in my head and I gasped for air.

"Mirella!" I heard them calling me, but my vision darkened, my hearing got muffled, and my legs became Jell-O.

I fell to the ground as tremors ran through my body, pain assaulted my head and chest, and hallucinations took over.

I was standing in the main square of Cora's and Rye's enclave, and alchemists ran toward me from the streets surrounding the square. I tried calling for my magic, but nothing happened. As they got close to me, the alchemists became dark shadows and flew up like smoke in the wind. But when their shadows were gone, I stared at the houses and buildings around me—they were on fire. I could hear the screams of the people inside the houses, begging for help. I tried moving, I tried running to them, but my legs wouldn't obey. It was like my feet were cemented to the ground. A loud roar echoed through the square, sending a shiver down my spine. I glanced over my shoulder and saw the dragon perched on top of the main building. It looked straight at me. I could swear it smiled before opening his big mouth and breathing fire.

Right at me.

Panic ceased my chest and all I could was crouch down and pray Saint Sara-la-Kali would save me.

The fire parted, and from the embers, Damara stepped to me.

She put a hand on her waist. "It's only going to get worse, you know." I couldn't answer. My voice wouldn't come out. "Your visions. They will be your death." What did she mean? Her lips spread into one of her wicked witch smiles. "Ask the elder council. Ask why you're feeling so much pain and having visions. They know the answer. But even if you ask, they won't answer. Because it's a secret, and they will do everything in their power to keep it a secret."

"Mirella!"

I blinked and everything was gone. Damara, the fire, the dragon, the main square. The pain, the dizziness, the darkness.

I was on the dirt ground of the old parking lot in front of Cora's and Rye's enclave. My friends were all around me, worry stamped on their faces.

Knelt beside me, Artan held my shoulders. "Mirella, answer me."

I pushed up. His hands dropped. "What happened?" I asked, confused.

"You just fell and started convulsing," Ellie said. Tears brimmed her eyes. "You scared us."

Ryane, knelt on my other side, reached for my wrist and checked my pulse. "Your heartbeat is slowing down now."

"I'm fine." I shot up, but wobbled on my feet. Artan caught my elbow and steadied me. He gave me an oh-really stare. "I'm fine, really."

"What was that, then?" Cora asked.

"It was like whatever you had before at the gas station, wasn't it?" Sloan asked.

"Are you sick?" Tomas asked.

"I-I don't think so." I offered them a grin, but it felt too fake even to me. "I'll figure it out once we get home."

Because I would confront the elder council about it. I wasn't sure what was happening, if I was really seeing Damara, if these were visions or hallucinations, but either way, the council had to have answers. If it was Damara, and she was lying to me, perhaps the council could help me find a way to keep her out of my head. If it was really her and she wasn't lying, then the council could still help me to keep her out of my head, but they would hear some nasty things from me until they told me the truth. If it was all in my head ... again, I would trust the council to know what to do. After all, I might not like them much, but they were supposed to be the most noble and knowledgeable tziganes from the entire enclave.

"What if it happens again while we're here?" Theron

asked. He stood several feet away, but his body and face were rigid. I hated seeing him like this.

"Then you all restrain me," I said.

"What if we're fighting?"

"Then just drop me somewhere I can't hurt anyone and do whatever you have to do." I held on to his stare. I didn't know why the hell he was treating me like that. It wasn't fair. I wasn't guilty of anything. His father and my mother had been the one sneaking around. My mother had a kid behind everyone's back. His father and my mother kept the secret—one for much longer than the other. If he wanted to be mad at someone, then he could direct that anger toward the real culprits.

I gritted my teeth, intent on giving him a piece of my mind.

Artan cleared his throat. "It's late. Going after Ramon now will only make everything worse. We must trust he got away from the dragon and is hiding for now. At first light, we'll search for him."

Theron grunted before marching away. For a moment, I worried about where he was going, but I pushed those thoughts from my mind. He was being so harsh toward me. Right now, I wanted to be mean, too.

Ellie hooked her arm on mine. "Come on. Let's get our tent back up so we can get some rest."

"Rest sounds good," I admitted in a low voice.

Together, we all walked to the site of our previous camp. At first, we were all silent—the only sounds were the gentle whoosh of a cold breeze and the crunch of our boots over dry leaves and roots.

But a few minutes later, I heard them.

Whispers.

She's crazy.

She's doomed.

She's going crazy.

She's losing it.

She's going to kill one of them.

She's going to die, too.

The whispers filled my head, and I wasn't sure if it was my friends whispering it all around me, or if this was like the hallucinations, something only I could hear.

Regardless, one thing was for sure.

It seemed I was really going crazy.

18

____

INSIDE OUR TENT, I LAY BESIDE ELLIE, BUT I BARELY SLEPT. THE few times I was able to close my eyes, Damara visited me. In my dreams, she teased and taunted me, showing me her magnificent powers and places where she found the heart flower, and how I would never beat her.

"Better surrender now," she said.

Well, that was something that would never happen.

In the end, nobody slept much, because after our little adventure last night, we had gone to bed late, and we woke up right before the sun was up.

When I walked out of the tent, I stilled.

"Ramon!"

Seated beside the fire, he glanced at me over his shoulder. "Morning."

At that, the others stepped out of the tents, surprised to see Ramon back.

I sat beside him. "Are you okay?"

"I'm fine," he said, his voice low. "A little tired, but fine."

Taking Ramon's other side, Theron punched his brother's shoulder. "Never do that again, idiot."

Ramon rubbed his shoulder. "No hitting, man. I'm sore." Theron hit him again. "Hey!"

"Let's see if you learn not to be so heroic now," Theron said, his voice tight. He might try not showing it, but we all knew he had struggled with Ramon's disappearance last night.

Artan took a seat across the fire. "What happened to the dragon?"

"Felix and I were able to distract him," Ramon said. "He followed us for a while, but then we had to hide in a valley and wait it out. It took the dragon a while to give up on finding Felix and me, but eventually he left."

Frowning, I looked around. "Where's Felix?"

"I'll take you to him soon."

"What do you mean?"

Ramon sighed. "On our way back, we found a place ..." He shuddered. "Felix is there, waiting for us."

Artan stiffened. "What place?"

Ramon glanced toward Cora and Rye, then locked his eyes with Artan's. "I think you all should see it."

"Then take us there," Theron said.

Ramon shook his head. "Eat first. Trust me. You won't be able to eat after."

What did he mean by that? But Ramon didn't explain anything else. He just told us to hurry and eat so we could go.

This time, no one went out to buy food. We just ate the snacks we still had and called it breakfast. Hopefully, we would be done here soon. I needed real food.

Like the day before, we broke up camp and took our

things back to the van. Then, with the essentials—water and weapons—we set out through the forest after Ramon.

The tension around the group felt like a whip about to crack, and the silence was maddening. It was easy to get lost in my troubled mind. I needed a distraction. But everyone seemed so focused on their own thoughts, I decided to focus on keeping one foot in front of the other.

It took us an hour to hike up the hill and arrive at the place Ramon had told us about. He stopped at the edge of a valley and pointed down. "This way."

We went down what seemed like a path around the valley, until it opened into a big pit.

"What is this?" Artan asked, getting closer to the pit.

The smell filled my nose before I saw it.

Rot. Blood. Death.

I plugged my nose and spied over the edge of the pit.

Bones.

The pit was full with human bones.

Ellie turned around, ran to the nearest tree, and threw up. I saw Ryane fighting against the urge to throw up, too. I gagged a couple of times, but then sadness over the dead people overrode any other sense.

"W-what is this?" Cora asked, her voice low. Detached. She stared at the pit with wide eyes, and her usual tanned skin was now pale.

"Tziganes," Theron whispered.

Ramon nodded. "I believe these belonged to tziganes."

Rye's eyes filled with tears. "Tziganes from our enclaves."

"We don't know that for sure, not until we do a DNA test," Ramon said.

Cora took a step back. "It can't be."

Rye reached for her. "Cora."

But she took another step back. "No, it can't be. It can't."

Cora's hand trembled and the ground quavered with her. She didn't even notice she was using her powers.

"Cora, look at me," Rye said, taking two steps to her.

She shook her head and retreated from him. "No. No matter what you say. It can't be."

Tears streamed down her cheeks as she inhaled deeply, then spun on her heels and took off.

"Cora!" Rye shouted and ran after her.

"Rye, wait," Artan called.

Rye slowed down and glanced over his shoulder. His eyes were red with unshed tears. "What?"

"I know you want to go after Cora," Artan said. "We do too, but instead of taking off alone after her, let's look for her together. It'll be safer."

Rye grunted. "Fine."

In the end, Artan told Felix and Ramon to stay at the site in case Cora came back, while the rest of us went out in three groups: Ellie, Theron, and Rye were one group, Sloan, Tomas, and Ryane formed the second one, and Artan and I were another.

Despite the situation, I was sure Artan had divided the groups like that to be alone with me. If he tried anything, I would punch him before he got one word out.

But, other than calling Cora's name every couple minutes, we marched in silence. Which wasn't really good for my head. It allowed for too much time to think.

Why couldn't I have a normal day as the heart maiden? Why did everything have to be so agitated, so messy? Cora's letter, the mission, the lies to be able to go out on this mission, the alchemist attack at the rest stop, Ramon being kidnapped, then saving him and giving him a potion that transformed him into a werewolf. The ghost town enclave, the booby traps, the revelation that I was Theron's and Ramon's sister. There was also the dragon, and now the bone pit.

And how could I forget about my pains and the hallucinations? Since we had left the enclave, I had had three episodes, and during one of those, I had almost hurt Artan.

It was too much, just too much.

Once we found Cora, I would first hug her, then I would convince her it was time to go home. And once we were home, I would ask for a vacation. The elder council might laugh in my face, but I really needed some time where I was just Mirella, the twenty-year-old woman, not Mirella, the heart maiden. I knew they wouldn't let me go on a real vacation, but as long as I could lay on my couch, eat popcorn, and watch movies and tv shows all day, I didn't need much.

I let out a sigh. The way the elder council hated me, I doubted they would grant me one day off.

"Mirella." Artan's voice broke through my zooming thoughts. He grabbed my wrist and slowed down.

"What is it?" I asked, thinking he had seen something.

He stared at me with those deep amber eyes. "We need to talk."

19

"About?" I asked, already feeling on the defensive. Things hadn't been easy between Artan and me for the last couple of weeks, and when he approached me like this, I could only think it was about to get worse.

He let go of my wrist. "About—"

I glanced to the path ahead. "We should keep going."

"Mirella," Artan called my name like a prayer.

My heart squeezed.

I sucked in a sharp breath. "Artan, if you want, we can talk about Cora and finding her *while* we're actually looking for her. Anything else you might want to talk about, I'm out."

I started walking again.

Artan caught up with me. "All right, then let's talk about something else. Your headaches and those hallucinations."

I glared at him. "I thought I just said I would only talk about Cora and finding her."

"So you're just going to pretend nothing is wrong?"

I halted and turned to him. "Of course, something is

wrong. A lot. But I'm not about to let it affect our mission. Well, more than it's already messed things up."

"Since we left Lovell, you have had three episodes, Mirella. If that's not problematic, then I don't know what it is."

I flinched and took a step back. "I don't know what happened to you, but I would rather if we went back to *not* talking to each other."

Irritated, I marched off.

Artan stepped in front of me and blocked my way. "Mirella, please, listen to me. I'm just saying that because I care." He paused, his eyes intent on mine. "I care about you."

I closed my eyes for a moment as his words sent an avalanche of feelings inside me. How dare he say this to me? "Artan, you're engaged."

"To a woman I barely know and don't love. I didn't choose her. It was an arranged engagement."

"And to tziganes, that is sacred. You should try to keep her in your mind and your heart." Even though it hurt, I tried putting myself in Kizzy's shoes. If I were her, I would want my future husband to be faithful to me.

"There's someone else in my heart, Mirella." He reached for me. "You're in my heart."

"Please, don't say that." I kept my hands behind my back, so he wouldn't be able to touch them. "Besides, you know we can't, Artan." I told myself that all the time, in the hopes that it would finally sink in, and I would feel better. It hadn't worked so far. "The elder council killed Damara's lover. I won't be with someone and risk having them killed."

"I can defend myself," he said, his voice taking a hard edge. "And my *dat* and *puri daj* are part of the council. They would probably punish me, but not kill me."

"And you want to risk that?"

He was serious when he said, "For you, yes."

I shook my head. "Artan, don't do this." I grasped for any excuse I could think of, because if I didn't, I would give in to him. "Think about your honor. Until a couple of weeks ago, your honor was the most important thing. You should honor your commitment to your fiancée, and you should honor the rule about not touching the heart maiden."

Artan grasped my shoulders. "I'm touching the heart maiden. I *want* to touch the heart maiden. My honor is bound to you. That's all that matters to me."

Stunned, I didn't move as he tugged me to him and crashed his mouth on mine. But once his warm lips moved against mine, I lost it. I lost it all. I lost my mind. I lost the will to fight. I melted into his arms and parted my lips for him. Winding his arms around me and holding me tight, Artan deepened the kiss.

A shiver rolled down my spine and went all the way to my toes. I clung to him, suddenly wondering why I had resisted for so long. Why had we been arguing? Because when he kissed me, the rest of the world melted away.

At least for a few minutes.

But I couldn't erase all the worry bouncing inside my head.

My heart hurting, I broke the kiss and pushed him away. "We shouldn't be doing this."

"Are you serious? After that kiss, after kissing me back like that, are you going to deny your feelings for me?"

I shook my head. "I never denied my feelings for you, but you are still engaged to someone else."

He held on to me. "Mirella, don't push me away again."

My head spun; my heart squeezed. How could I feel so

confused? I knew what the right thing to do was, so why couldn't I do it? "I'm not. Not yet. I need time. I think we both need time."

"But—"

"I promise you we'll talk about this again, but right now, we have other matters that need our attention. We need to find Cora and get home. After we're safe in Lovell, we can talk. For real."

Until then, I would, hopefully, be able to raise the walls around my heart again and keep them there, no matter what he said or the way he looked at me.

But one thing I was sure of, I couldn't let him kiss me again. Once he kissed me, I lost all control.

Artan let out a long breath. "Okay. You're right. We can do that."

Pushing away all feelings and thoughts related to Artan from my mind and chest, I looked around. We could choose any direction to go. It didn't matter. Taking the lead, Artan resumed the march through the forest. As if I could raise an invisible shield around me, around my heart and soul, I inhaled deeply and followed him.

"I'm worried about her," I admitted after a few steps. "I really had hoped the letter was real."

"I know. All of us hoped that, I guess." He frowned. "But I can't wrap my head around something."

"What?"

He glanced at me. "It seems the letter was fake, but so far, we haven't encountered anything concrete that indicate it was a trap. But we've been here for two days and the alchemists haven't shown their faces. Was it really a trap? If it wasn't, then who sent the letter?"

"I've been wondering the same thing." And there was the

other journal in her house, which had been burned to the ground. Despite crispy edges, the journal was fine.

What about the booby traps around the enclave? Cora and Rye insisted there weren't any booby traps when they lived here, which meant they were installed after. By whom? Alchemists trying to catch us, or tziganes who survived?

Nothing made sense.

And there was the dragon, too. The monster seemed to like to stroll around the enclave and collect random objects. With a dragon around, who would stay?

Another puzzling piece was the bone pit. I could only assume those were the bodies of the tziganes who had perished when the enclave was attacked. But who had moved the bodies to that pit. And why?

I mentioned those to Artan and he was as clueless as I was. However, it was clear there was nothing for us here. We had to find Cora, get our group together, and go back home.

I knew Cora and Rye would be devastated after being filled with hope, but maybe I could do something for them. I bet their families didn't have a proper send-off ceremony. I would talk to the elder council and do a proper ceremony for them—the passing ritual.

I was so deep in thought I almost didn't feel it, but once I focused and sent my senses out, it was too strong to ignore. A dark, heavy cloud surrounded Artan and me.

I slowed down. "Alch—"

"I know," Artan whispered. He stiffened. "I just felt them."

"What do we do?" I asked, tensing. With my senses, I couldn't count them, but I knew it wasn't one or two or three. And there was only Artan and me here.

Stepping closer to me, Artan whispered, "Mirella, be ready to fight."

20

———

They stepped out from the trees' shadows all at the same time. Ten alchemists with the black mask over the lower part of their faces and holding their shadow swords— the normal kind of alchemists we were used to.

Holding his sword out, Artan pulled me behind him, but the alchemists had us surrounded.

One of the alchemists stepped forward. He took off his mask, revealing his pale face and black lips. "We've been having fun, but it's time to end this."

Artan pointed his sword at the alchemist. "What are you talking about?"

"Our game," he said simply. "It has been too easy. Much easier than I thought it would go."

I spied the alchemist from behind Artan. "W-what do you mean?"

"The letter. We sent the letter to your friend in the hopes that she would bring you to us."

My mouth hit the floor.

"So it was a trap," Artan said through gritted teeth.

Calm, the alchemist nodded. "It was."

I frowned. "But ... how did you find her father's code?"

"And why wait two days to attack us?" Artan asked.

The alchemist paced in front of us, his steps measured, firm. "When we attacked this enclave, I found a tzigane hiding the journals. That caught my attention, of course. So I killed him and took the journals."

My stomach dropped. This man killed Cora's father.

Artan snorted. "It took you three years to decipher the code?" What was that a condescending tone? Was he mocking the alchemist? Right now, when we had several swords pointed at us?

"No, that was not what took us this long." He shifted his black eyes to me. "We were waiting for something else for an entirely different reason. And when we found her, I can say I was glad that she was good friends with the only survivors from our attack." He tilted his head. "I knew we could infect your friend, but I thought it would be hard to convince you."

"What do you mean infect?" I asked, my voice catching.

"Isn't your friend acting strange lately? A little more agitated and eager and forward than usual?" His black lips stretched into a sick grin. "There was a little elixir in the ink we used to write the code. The more she touched the letter, the surer she would be of its authenticity, and the more excited and pushy she would become to find out the truth."

I gasped. I had noticed she was acting different, but I thought it was because of the circumstances, not because of some elixir.

"Why not attack us once we got here?" Artan asked again.

"What's the fun in that?" The alchemists shrugged. "Haven't you seen all the booby traps? All part of our game."

"You're sick," I spat.

He ignored me and went on. "We wanted to see you suffering as you went through an enclave we decimated." He took a step closer. "Just like we're going to do with your enclave once we're done with you."

The alchemists lunged at us.

On instinct, I moved my hands up and a fire wall appeared in front of us. But the shield wouldn't hold for long.

"We should run," I said.

Artan shook his head. "We won't get far before they are on us again."

But what was the alternative? To fight them? There were too many for just the two of us.

I didn't have an opportunity to come up with a plan as my shield broke into tiny flames that disappeared into the air.

The alchemists advanced on us. Artan engaged in a sword fight with a few of them, while I used my magic to keep the rest back.

But when the leader stepped forward holding a green stone—exactly like the one Ellie had been holding when she delivered me to the alchemists a few months ago—my magic flickered. Grunting, I called for it, but with the power of the green gem, I couldn't even hold on to it.

I stepped back, realizing I wouldn't be able to fight them if they took away my magic.

Desperate, I turned around to grab Artan and run, but ended up face-to-face with another alchemist. The masked man pulled his arm back, aiming the shadow sword right at me. I froze, knowing that even if I moved, I wouldn't be fast enough, not this time.

The blade came at me.

Artan jumped in front of me.

The blade went deep into his stomach.

"No!" I cried. Panic took over my senses, and my magic faded from my veins.

Groaning, Artan pressed a hand to his stomach and knelt on the ground. I crouched beside him.

He smiled at me. "I'm sorry ... I couldn't protect you."

I cupped his face. "No, no, no. Stay with me. You'll be fine." I pressed a hand over his wound, but blood seeped between our fingers. "Stay with me."

A sob raked through my body.

Hands closed around my shoulders and pulled me back.

"No," Artan rasped.

I jerked and screamed as the alchemists carried me away from Artan, their grips like steel. I tried calling my magic, but I wasn't sure if it was the panic exploding inside me that prevented me from reaching it, or the alchemist's stone.

"Let me go," I cried.

All the alchemists retreated with me.

All but one.

One alchemist stayed beside Artan. The man watched me as he lifted his sword high.

My heart stopped.

The alchemists carrying me went down the hill, and I lost sight of Artan.

"No," I whispered.

I couldn't believe it. I couldn't even think about it, because it didn't make sense. Artan was one of the strongest warriors Lovell and Bellville had, if not the strongest. He couldn't die this easily. This simply.

But the blade had pierced him deep, and he was losing too much blood.

One alchemist had stayed behind with him, preparing to kill him.

For all I knew, Artan was gone.

21

My body and mind were numb. I didn't know what was up and down. I had forgotten how to breathe. And it only got worse once the alchemists blindfolded me and tied my hands behind my back.

It was like I was floating down a river made of oil. It was so thick and slick, I couldn't move a muscle. I just let it take me to the waterfall, where I knew I would fall. Where I would end.

I didn't know how long the alchemists carried me through the forest—I had also lost all sense of time.

But my heartbeat picked up when a new sense pushed against me.

Who was ...?

"Get them!" an alchemist cried.

At first, the alchemists carrying me sped off, trying to get away from whoever was attacking, but soon they put me down to fight.

Blindfolded, I only heard the grunts, the stomps, and the sounds of metal slicing flesh.

As long as it wasn't any more of my friends getting hurt, I could stomach it.

I hoped.

Curled on the cold ground, I focused on my magic. I called on it; I begged it to come back to me. Tears filled my eyes as I promised to never let panic get the best of me again.

A flicker started deep in my chest. I tended to it, and slowly, the flicker grew into a spark, then into a flame, and soon it was a violent river running through my veins.

I channeled my magic to my arms and wrists and burned the ropes. The smell of crispy rope filled my nostrils just as they broke.

I took the blindfold off.

Just a couple of steps from me, Cora swiped her sword wide, cutting the throat of an alchemist, and to her left, Rye plunged his sword into the chest of another one.

Their bodies fell to the ground with a sickening thud.

No alchemists left, Cora and Rye turned to me.

"Mi!" Cora rushed to me. "Are you all right?"

She hooked her arm around my elbow and helped me stand.

Tears filled my eyes and I shook my head. "No."

"What happened?" Rye asked.

"Artan ... the alchemists got Artan." A sob ripped through me.

Rye frowned. "What do you mean?"

I shook my head. I couldn't even think about it, much less say it.

Cora hugged me. "Oh, Mi."

Rye stiffened. "I should go after him."

"No." Cora pulled away, but kept one arm firmly around me. "I told you, when I was wandering alone, I found alchemists. I hid from them and heard them talking. They are spread around the forest, looking for us. If you're alone when they find you ..."

As much as I would love Rye to go find Artan, even if it was only way to bring his body with us, I knew Cora was right. Now wasn't the time to wander alone through the forest. We had to stick together. At least until we dealt with the alchemists. Then ... then we could go back and find Artan.

"We need to find the others," I said.

"You're right." Rye nodded. He reached for me. "Do you need help walking?"

Shaking my head, I disentangled myself from Cora. "No, I'm fine. Still a little shocked and numb but fine."

The three of us moved through the forest, sending our senses out every couple of minutes, wary of any alchemists. I only hoped they hadn't gotten to the rest of my friends yet. It hurt too much to think about what happened to Artan. I couldn't bear it if anyone else was hurt.

All of it was because of me. Theron was right. The trap had been set through Cora, but I had been the one who lied to the elder council and brought them here. If I hadn't lied, if maybe I had investigated a little more before we launched into this crazy mission, Artan would be fine.

Tears filled my eyes, and I swallowed the pain lodged in my throat.

I would cry a river for him, but later. My tears had to wait until later. First, I had to get to my friends and fight the alchemists.

A mirror image of Cora, Rye, and myself flashed in my mind two seconds before Felix appeared between the trees.

He rushed to us, and behind him were Theron, Ramon, and Ellie.

Theron looked around. "Where's Artan?"

"Where's Sloan, Tomas, and Ryane?" I asked.

Ellie's lips trembled. "They were taken by the alchemists."

22

AN INVISIBLE HOLE OPENED AT MY FEET, AND I FELL INTO THAT black abyss.

It couldn't be.

We couldn't lose any more of our friends.

"They were taken? Alive?" Cora asked.

"We're not sure," Ramon said. "We arrived too late, but it seems they fought a group of alchemists and were taken."

"They will use them as bait," Theron said, his tone serious. Business-like. "To lure us to them."

Another trap. I pushed all doubt and fear from within and focused on revenge. I was going to take all these alchemists down and save my friends.

"It doesn't matter," I said out loud. "Artan is gone. I won't let it happen to anyone else."

Ellie's eyes bugged. "What do you mean Artan is gone?"

"He's dead?" Theron asked.

New tears burned the back of my eyes, but I blinked fast. "I don't know! He was stabbed while saving me, then I was dragged away. I saw one alchemist with him. He had his sword ..." My voice broke.

"If he were alive, the alchemists would have taken him to where Sloan, Tomas, and Ryane are," Rye said.

"But even if he wasn't alive," Theron said, "the alchemists would have taken his body to drain his blood."

My stomach turned. I couldn't go into a fight with that image in my mind. "Please, can we not talk about that right now?"

"Right." Theron straightened. "Let's just hope Artan is still alive and was taken to where the others are."

"Does anyone know where they are?" Ellie asked.

Felix growled.

"I think he can follow their scents," I translated.

Ramon looked at the lion. "Show us the way."

Without hesitation, Felix turned and we set out after him.

With each step we took, my chest hurt more. By Saint Sara-la-Kali, Artan was gone. Oscar and Darcy would right out kill me for his death.

I could barely focus on following Felix and my friends, much less send out my senses every few minutes, like everyone else was doing, trying to prepare ourselves in case we encountered more alchemists.

About thirty minutes into our trek, I sensed something weird.

I halted and sent more of my magic out, trying to find what was going on.

Ramon glanced at me over his shoulder. "What happened?"

The group slowed down and looked at me.

A warm feeling bloomed in my chest. "I think ..."

I gasped and ran back.

"Mirella!" Theron yelled.

Blind to the forest, I followed the little thread. I only halted when he came into view.

Artan.

One hand over his wound, the other on a tree's trunk as he leaned into it for support.

He lifted his sweaty face and offered me a small smile. "Hi."

Emotion burst into me and I ran to him. He stumbled into me and I hugged him. It was all I could so we both didn't go tumbling down to the ground.

"How ... what ...?" I didn't know what to ask first.

"Did you think I would go down that easy? The moment that alchemist lifted his sword to strike me, I moved. I found my sword and killed him." He groaned as he pulled back. He had ripped a piece of his sleeve and it tied around his waist. "This damn thing slowed me down, though."

I wanted to call his sister to heal him, at least a little since she wasn't a full scale healer, but she wasn't here. By Saint Sara-la-Kali, I had to tell him that his sister, his future brother-in-law, and his cousin had been taken.

But first, we had to do something about his wound. If he kept bleeding like this, he would go into shock. And when we found Ryane and Tomas and Sloan and had to fight, he wouldn't last a minute.

I placed my hand over his wound and called my magic. I wasn't a healer and couldn't do much, but so far I had found out my magic could do things I didn't expect it to. I poured every ounce of my feelings and hopes and desires into my magic.

Please, heal him, I begged.

Artan hissed, and I pulled my hand away. He grabbed my

hand and put it in place. "Keep going. I think it's working." I wasn't sure what he meant, but I kept going. He hissed more and more, until he stopped. "It's done."

He unwrapped the cloth from around his waist and lifted his torn armor. The wound was cauterized, as if my fire had done that. It didn't look pretty with an ugly red scar. "I'm sorry that is all I could do."

"Are you kidding me? You might have just saved me," he said, with a soft smile.

"But now you'll have a scar."

"Don't worry about it. I'm sure my *puri daj* can lessen it a little. And if she can't ..." He shrugged. "Tokens of battle. Trophies of a soldier."

"What happened?" Theron asked from behind us.

Finally, the rest of the group had found us. I hadn't even noticed I had run so fast to make them lose my trail.

"Sorry I took off like that." I gestured to Artan. "But I found something."

"Artan," Cora breathed. "You're all right?"

He nodded. "I am now."

Ramon pressed the group. "If you're well, then we should get going."

Artan's brows curled down. "Going where? Where's Ryane, Tomas, and Sloan?"

Theron and Ellie looked away, Ramon's and Rye's faces fell, Cora's eyes filled with tears, Felix let out a sorrowful growl.

I inhaled deeply before saying, "The alchemists took them."

Artan's entire body tensed. "W-what?"

"We're going after them now," Theron said.

"Then let's go!" Artan urged. He gritted his teeth and pushed through any residual pain.

Felix assumed the front of the group again and he led us through the forest. To me, it all looked the same. If we were going in circles and nobody told me, I would never know. But I was sure Felix knew exactly where to go.

It didn't take long for Felix to take us through a hidden path around a small hill. On the other side, the hill was rocky, and down below, there was a hidden clearing. From the middle of the path, we couldn't see the clearing well yet, but from the images Felix projected in my mind, I knew that was where we were going.

We approached the clearing, hiding behind tree trunks and watching for alchemist.

My heart squeezed at the sight we found.

"By Saint Sara-la-Kali," Cora whispered from my side, echoing my shock.

Alchemists littered the clearing, going to and from a long table set up in the center, where vials and pots were spread out. On the corner of the table, a dark red liquid bubbled inside a big black pot resembling an archaic cauldron.

On the other side of the table, there were three chairs. Ryane, Tomas, and Sloan were tied to the chairs. This time, there were no IVs sticking in their arms. No. The alchemists here had been crueler. They made several cut on their arms and let their blood seep out and into bowls set on the ground underneath their hands.

An alchemist approached Ryane. He ran a finger on one of her cuts. Then, he licked her blood from his fingertip.

My stomach turned.

Beside me, Artan groaned. "I can't just watch."

And just like that, he drew his sword from the scabbard at his waist and marched into the clearing.

"Artan, no!" Theron rasped.

The alchemists saw the moment Artan stepped from behind the trees and approached them. Half of them turned back to whatever they were doing, as if Artan wasn't much more than a fly they could swat away. The other half extended their arms, and the shadow swords appeared in their hands.

"Shit," Ramon cursed.

Channeling my magic, I glanced at my friends. "Let's do this."

23

FACING OFF WITH THE ALCHEMISTS, MY FRIENDS AND I STOOD A few steps behind Artan.

A low hiss echoed through the alchemists, as if they were wild animals that had gotten excited upon seeing their next meal.

The alchemists parted, and an unmasked one stepped forward. It was the same alchemist who had gotten Artan and me earlier.

He narrowed his dark eyes at Artan. "Didn't we kill you?"

"You tried," Artan said with a bite. "Now, let them go before I do to you what I did to the poor alchemist you left behind to finish me off."

"Such anger. I like that." The alchemist's black lips spread into a nasty grin. "But don't worry. All the anger and desire for revenge won't help today."

I joined Artan and faced the alchemist. "What is it that you want?"

He opened his arms to the side. "What every alchemist wants. Tzigane blood."

"I bet there is at least one other enclave much closer than ours. You could have gone to them without luring us here."

"You're smart," he said. "We'll always want tzigane blood, but we need something else."

"What is it?" Artan asked.

"Ah, it's a long story," the alchemist said. The coldness in his voice, the detached grin on his face, the depthless eyes, it all sent a shiver down my spine.

"We don't have time for a long story," Artan said. "Make it short."

"You're no fun." The alchemist tsked. "Long story short? We were the ones who attacked the enclave three years ago." He pointed to our right, the general direction of the enclave. "After we killed the tziganes and took them away to drain their blood, we searched through the rubble for anything useful. Like us, tziganes also make powerful potions, don't you?" He tilted his head in an odd angle. "We found lots of half-burned books containing instructions for spells and elixirs. One of them seemed quite interesting, but we made it even more interesting by changing it up a little. Instead of being a healing potion, we added a few special ingredients, and it suddenly became an elixir that grants immortality."

I gasped. "You succeeded?"

"We haven't had the opportunity to test it yet," he said. "Because it needs the blood of a half dozen tziganes and the blood of the heart maiden."

Artan shot an arm in front of me, as if he could keep me safe just like that. "You're dreaming."

"We honestly thought we would never be able to make it since there hasn't been a heart maiden in over two hundred years." His dark eyes shone as he fixed them on me. "Imagine my surprise when you showed up, and you were friends with the only three survivors of this enclave."

"You sent the letter," Cora muttered from behind me.

The alchemist looked at her. "Like I said, we searched the entire enclave for things we could use. For some reason, I held on to the journals with code I had found. I'm glad they came in handy after all."

Cora's knuckles turned white as she gripped the hilt of her sword tight. "You'll never succeed."

"But we're almost done." He gestured to the cauldron at the table. "All we need is your blood." He extended his hand to his side, and the shadow sword pop up on his hand. "All you have to do is surrender."

"Never!" Cora yelled.

The alchemist shook his head. "I'll give you one more chance." He stepped to the side and the crowd behind him parted, giving us a perfect view of Ryane, Tomas, and Sloan— and the alchemists holding their shadow swords to their throats.

"No," Artan breathed.

"Don't listen to them!" Tomas shouted. He was the only one still conscious, but his skin was pale. He was losing blood fast.

The alchemist lifted his finger. The swords against Ryane's, Tomas's and Sloan's throat moved a hairsbreadth. "Your choice."

Grunting, Artan's shoulders sagged. Eyes downcast, he dropped his sword on the ground.

I gawked at him. What the hell was he doing? Was he really giving up? If we did, then there was no chance to make it out of here alive. But if we didn't—

"You win," Artan said, his voice dejected.

Whispers of protests started among our friends.

Then, in the blink of an eye, Artan threw his hands out and sent a strong gust of wind forward. It weaved up and down as it crossed the clearing, until it curled under Ryane's and Tomas's and Sloan's chairs, coming up fast. The alchemists lost their grips and the shadow swords flew away.

The leader turned to us and bared his teeth. "You little …"

"Now!" Artan yelled. He kicked his sword with the toe of his boot, enough to make it lift from the ground, then he hooked his foot under it and propelled it high. He caught it with his hand, just in time to swing it wide and strike the chest of the alchemist running toward him.

The leader raised his sword and yelled, "Get the heart maiden!"

The alchemists who had been working on the potion stopped and joined the other half, ready to fight us. Almost all of them turned to me.

"Protect Mirella," Theron said, coming to stand beside me. I blinked at him, momentarily surprised that he had said that. I thought he hated my guts at the moment.

"I'm going to get Ryane, Tomas, and Sloan," Artan said in a low growl.

"I'll help you," Ramon said before taking off his shirt and wolfing out.

The two of them rushed through the alchemists, while Theron, Cora, Rye, and Felix stayed by my side and fought off the alchemists who advanced on us. Meanwhile, Ellie ducked behind us, shaking with fear.

I really needed to take her to fighting lessons with me. Perhaps she could learn a move or two and be more helpful in the future.

I kicked myself for thinking about the future, when the

present seemed so messy. Focus on the task at hand—fighting alchemists.

My power hummed in my veins and I let it out.

Theron and Rye cut through the alchemists with their swords. Cora opened holes and sent earth rocks flying at our enemies. With his claws and sharp teeth, Felix ripped many throats. And I used my fire. I threw fire bolts and raised fire walls when necessary.

But, even though we were strong, there were too many alchemists around us, and they weren't playing fair. Potions hit the ground around us every five seconds. From dizziness smoke, to convulsing spells, and numbing potions, the alchemists were trying everything to stop us without hurting us too much.

After all, they needed our blood. If we bled out before the fighting ended, then it was all in vain.

I conjured a snake of fire and sent it to the alchemist rushing at me. The snake found his legs and coiled around his body. It tightened and burned. The alchemist cried as the fire spread over his body and burned him alive.

I turned my face, hating the sight. I did it only because it was them or us, and I would fight for us until my last breath.

Another alchemist swung his sword at me. I ducked, then whirled back, gaining some distance from him. I conjured another snake of fire and—

The alchemist sidestepped, allowing another one to come forward. He threw a vial at me. It broke against my legs, spreading black liquid on my uniform.

Looking down, I stepped back. "What the hell?" I was about to send my fire snake at him when I felt it. The potion on my legs working.

My skin underneath the uniform prickled, my insides

curled, my muscles contracted. I fell on my knees as little tremors ran down my body. The magic flickered and faded.

The alchemist laughed. "Not so tough now, are you?"

"W-what is this?" I asked, my voice a thin shrill.

"A debilitating spell," he said. "It'll make you dizzy and weak, and you won't be able to use your magic."

The first alchemist who distracted stepped to his side. "Making it easier for us to take you."

"No, no." I tried scooting away, but I barely moved an inch when they hooked their hands under my arms and hauled me up.

"Mirella!" Ellie yelled. She took a step forward.

"No!" I cried to her. "Stay with Theron."

After parrying an attack, Theron's eyes flickered between Ellie and me. "By Saint Sara-la-Kali ..."

The alchemists pulled me back, toward where I had last seen the chairs with Ryane, Tomas, and Sloan. I fought against the spell, but it was too strong. I didn't have any control over my legs, and I couldn't channel my magic.

Damn it!

I took a second to look around and analyze the situation. Everything was a mess. Theron tried to protect Ellie while fighting wave after wave of alchemists, and now he kept eyeing me too, as if he was trying to come up with a plan to get me back. Beside him, Cora alternated between using her earth magic and her sword as she fought our enemies. Rye was a couple of feet ahead of her, slashing his sword right and left, cutting the alchemists who dared to come close. Felix did the same, but he used his claws and teeth. The poor lion tried moving toward me, but there were too many alchemists around him, and for every inch he gained, he soon lost two.

And on the other side of the clearing, Artan and wolf

Ramon fought alchemists around the chairs where Ryane and Sloan sat. Tomas's ropes had been cut, and he knelt on the ground behind Artan, trying to recover.

There were too many alchemists, and we weren't progressing fast enough. If we didn't cut through them soon, I didn't think we would have a chance here.

I glanced at my friends and caught Ellie stealing glances at the table in the center of the clearing. I could see the wheels turning in her head as she came up with the plan. And was ready to execute it.

"Ellie, no!" I yelled.

Too late. She dashed through the alchemists, dodging them with ease—she was small and they hadn't expected her to run past them. Their attention had been at the tziganes, not at the cowering *gadjo* girl.

Without slowing down, Ellie bumped the table.

And pushed the cauldron, tipping it over the table and spilling the potion on the ground. Heavy, dark smoke rose from the dried grass.

"No!" the alchemist leader yelled.

For a moment, the fighting paused as everyone looked at the cauldron and its spilled contents.

But Artan and Theron were too smart. Knowing that one second could be our salvation, they moved before everyone else. Theron ran to Ellie, while Artan freed Ryane and caught her in his arms.

The leader advanced on Ellie, who was shaking her hands as if she had burned them, but then Theron reached her. He grabbed her arm and pulled her behind him, while he swung his sword wide and drew a line across the leader's chest.

The leader faltered and Theron finished him.

Again, the fighting paused.

Meanwhile, Artan carted Ryane to us, Tomas coming right behind him, and Ramon bit off the ropes around Sloan's legs and chest. Still faint, Sloan slid to the ground. Ramon stayed in front of him, fending off alchemists who advanced on both.

With his air magic, Artan pushed back the alchemists on his way, and he brought Ryane to where Rye, Cora, and Ellie were. Tomas practically fell on the ground beside them. Meanwhile, I pushed over the table. Without being able to move my legs, I couldn't do much. I rolled over the table and tried to scoot to the other side, but alchemists held my arms and tied them behind my back.

"Behave and we won't hurt your friends," one alchemist said.

"Much," a second one added with a sneer.

As if I believed them.

They rushed to pick up whatever they could from the broken vials and the spilled potion, even if it was a tiny drop. Could they still finish it with only one drop?

By Saint Sara-la-Kali, I hoped they didn't.

I called on my magic, but only a spark answered. I tried coaxing that spark, make it bigger, but their damn potion was working. My magic had faded and I couldn't call on it. Without magic, I jerked my shoulders, trying to loosen the ropes around my wrists. It seemed like a fool's errand.

Spinning and cutting through the alchemists, Artan made his way back to Ramon and Sloan. But as he approached them, three alchemists advanced on Ramon at once. He fended them off, but one called his shadow sword and slashed Ramon's hind leg. The wolf let out a yelp as he limped back.

"No!" I whispered, watching it all unfold around me and not being able to help. I felt useless.

With Ramon a few feet back, the alchemists grabbed Sloan by the hair and pulled him up. Half-awake, Sloan groaned and jerked, but he went still when a shadow sword rested against his neck.

"Stop right there," the alchemist holding the sword said to Artan, who stared at his cousin with wide eyes. "One more step and he dies."

My stomach twisted in knots.

"And no air tricks, pretty boy," one of the alchemists said.

Frozen in place, Artan dropped his sword and raised his hands. "What do you want?"

"We want you all dead," the alchemist said with a laugh.

He pulled the sword back, slashing across Sloan's throat.

"No," I whispered as my breath caught. My chest seized in pain.

"No!" Artan screamed, falling to his knees.

The alchemist let go of Sloan, and his body hit the ground with a loud thud. They stepped over Sloan and advanced toward Artan.

Tears filled my eyes.

By Saint Sara-la-Kali, where did it all go so wrong? Why? Ellie burned her hands, Ryane was unconscious from blood loss, Tomas didn't look much better than her, Ramon had injured his leg, and now Sloan was dead.

Sloan was dead.

And next would be Artan.

That was enough.

In the blink of an eye, rage swept through me, powerful and constant, replacing my shock and hurt. I welcomed it, I encouraged it, I used it.

Embracing this new feeling, I searched deep and called my magic.

It came forward like wildfire.

Burning through the ropes around my wrist felt as easy as breathing. In no time, the alchemists' potion was gone. It evaporated from my body or burned away, I didn't care. It was gone, and I could now move.

Summoning my fire, I jumped off the table.

My feet touched the ground and fire spread. It spread through me, from me. The alchemists jumped back, wary of the fire. I walked to the center of the crowd, each of my steps leaving a dark mark on the ground.

Once more the fighting stopped, and this time all eyes were on me.

The fire took over my legs, my chest, my arms. I opened my hands and looked around the alchemists. "Leave now or burn."

They flinched, but didn't move.

I moved my arms in an arc, and my fire flew toward them like a long, deadly whip. They jumped back, but a few were caught. The whip licked their arms or chests or backs and fire spread. In seconds, they were on the ground, jerking and screaming as my fire took over their entire bodies and burned them alive.

"Last chance," I said, my voice eerie. Creepy. Not mine.

Most of the alchemists ran. A handful stayed and stood their ground. I sent my fire whip to them. They moved, trying to get away from its path, but my fire molded to my will and it went after them. The tip of whip hit most of the alchemists, and they burned in matter of seconds.

Only three alchemists were left standing.

I smirked at them. "You asked for it." Twirling my arm, I sent out the fire whip again.

The three of them scurried away like scared rats.

All the alchemists were gone. They were either dead or running away. I was a little stunned they actually ran and left everything behind. The table, the broken vials, their tools.

They simply ran.

Away from me.

I closed my eyes and sucked in a long breath, and my fire retreated into me. I compressed it in my chest, as if I was cradling it with both my hands. When it was no more than a spark, again, I let go of my breath and opened my eyes.

My friends watched me with wide eyes. Wary of me. Maybe even scared.

My shoulders sagged. "We won," I whispered, feeling like I had only lost.

Snow started falling, as if trying to quell, to hide, everything that had happened there.

The tension and silence were suffocating inside the van as we made our way back to the enclave. A trip that was supposed to be nine hours long, would take only seven because of Theron's heavy foot—even with the snow falling hard. If he could, he would have gone even faster, since some of us needed the help of an experienced healer.

Ramon had bandaged his leg and stopped the bleeding. With his new super healing, he would be okay, without even a scar to tell the tale. Ellie had her burned hands wrapped in a cloth with some crude healing paste Artan had brought. It wouldn't heal the burn, but it would make it bearable until we got back to Lovell. I had closed the stab wound in Artan's stomach, but it had been hastily done. He would still need his grandmother to lessen the scar, and make sure there was no internal damage. Tomas was already recovering. He had been the last one strapped to the chair and the first one out. For some reason, he hadn't bled as much and had maintained his consciousness through the entire ordeal.

Then, there was Ryane. She was still weak from the blood

loss. She went in and out of consciousness too often. I used my powers to send warmth into her and keep her heart strong, but I wasn't sure how long she would be able to hang on.

The others had a few scratches and sore muscles and pure exhaustion, but they would survive.

Unlike Sloan.

Each time I thought about Sloan, my throat closed and my eyes filled with tears. I wished I could go back in time and do something. If I had had one more second, maybe I could have been able to see it coming and stop it before it happened. I could have saved him.

But I couldn't save him. Nobody could. Sloan was gone.

I glanced back to the last row. Sloan's body was there now, wrapped in our blankets. Artan watched over him, as if he could stare life back into his cousin.

Since I had shooed the alchemists away—or killed them. My stomach revolted with nausea just thinking about all the lives I had taken—Artan hadn't even looked my way. Seeing his despair over Sloan and worry about Ryane, I knew he now blamed me, too.

Everyone did.

After all, I had been the one to make this trip possible. It might not be the best excuse, but it was the only thing they could grab, the only thing that made sense right now. They were feeling angry and lost and confused.

And I was an easy target to blame. Especially because I didn't protest when Artan jerked away from my touch when I tried to hug him to comfort him about Sloan and Ryane, or when Theron yelled at me because of Ellie's injuries. Never mind that she had been the one to act and tip over the cauldron and get burned in the process. I had told her to stay away, but did they remember that?

No, of course not.

I didn't protest as they glared at me while we hopped in the van and got ready to go back.

I wouldn't protest.

I would take it all, I would accept it all, because I felt guilty.

There was someone else feeling guilty in this van. On the seat in front of me; Cora kept her head low the entire trip. From time to time, I could hear a couple of sniffs, which eased out when Rye put his arm around her shoulders and tugged her against his side.

A pang of jealousy cut through my heart.

I didn't have a single friend on my side right now.

Relief coursed through me once we arrived at Lovell in the middle of the night. Theron took the van through the gates and over the snow-covered roads, but once we hopped out and found the elder council waiting for us, my relief was gone.

Tears brimmed in my eyes when Sloan's mother and his fiancée saw his body and started crying. His mother screamed and his fiancée looked ready to die. I shrank into myself, afraid they would turn to me.

Darcy and Oscar fretted over Ryane. After a glare toward me, Darcy took Ryane to the infirmary with the help of another council member. Tomas went along to get checked. Theron followed them with Ellie.

Oscar stood tall and faced our group. "I expect all of you in the council room in twenty minutes." Then, he spun on his heels and stomped away.

Ramon grabbed my bag from the van and handed it

to me.

Frowning, I took it. Wasn't he going to yell at me too? I looked down at the improvised bandage around his thigh. "You should go to the infirmary, too."

Shrugging, he untied the bandage from around his leg. "It's all healed now." He picked up his bag and slung it across his shoulders. He gestured to the snow-covered path leading to the main square. "Shall we?"

I stared at him. "Are you sure you want to walk with me?"

One corner of his lips curled up. Like this, I could see how alike he and Theron really were. "I am."

We started our way to the main building where the council room was located, and I tried my best not to notice the agitation spreading through the enclave—everyone should be sleeping, since it was past three in the morning, but with the news of our return, Sloan's death, and Ryane's injuries, the enclave was as alive as during the day.

Soon, rumors about how it all went would spread faster than wildfire. It would get distorted and mixed up, and instead of being only blamed for what happened to them, I would be blamed for actually doing it. Who knew? I might have had the sword in my hand.

A shudder rolled down my spine.

"Don't let it all affect you," Ramon said, his voice low.

"Easier said than done."

"They will come around." He opened the door of the main building to me. "They are just hurt by all that happened. They need to find someone to blame."

"And I'm right here." I nodded as I walked inside the building. "I know, I thought about that already. But it still hurts."

He placed a heavy hand on my shoulder. "You did your

best. Remember, you're the one who saved us in the end. If you hadn't done that super fire magic, it's possible we would all be dead now."

His words brought new tears to my eyes and a new emotion to my heart. This was my brother—*my brother*—telling me I did well. I had never thought something like this could happen.

We were the first to arrive at the council meeting room, aside from the elders already seated on the other side of their semi-oval table. Only Darcy and Oscar were missing, probably because they were tending to Ryane.

Soon after, Cora, Rye, and Artan arrived. Artan stayed in the back, away from all of us. Then, with only a minute to spare, Theron and Ellie entered the room. Ellie had a real bandage around her hands now, and I could bet there was plenty of decent healing paste smeared across her skin.

At the twenty minute mark, Oscar came into the room through a back door.

He stopped by his seat and said, "We'll wait on my *daj*. She should be here soon."

I tried relaxing while we waited, but I felt the prick of the glares from the council members and from my friends on my skin.

Finally, almost fifteen minutes later, Darcy rushed into the room. She looked tired and nervous, as if she had used too much magic and needed some rest.

We all needed rest. Besides fighting for our lives, we hadn't slept in almost twenty hours, and we hadn't eaten in almost as long.

"I will get directly to the point," Darcy said. She remained standing before her chair. "The elder council is disappointed by all the lies associated with this mission. Because of those lies, my *puri chey* Ryane is in a critical state and my *puri chini* Sloan is gone." Her lower lip trembled, and I felt bad for the old hag. I hated her, but I never wished loss on anyone. "And a tzigane became a *ruv*." Her gaze fell on Ramon. He held his head high, not afraid of her. "I don't know what this will mean for you or for us. We need to investigate how your transformation will affect your tzigane blood. Just know that the enclave is our priority. If you turning into a *ruv* puts any tzigane in danger, we'll have to act."

Ramon nodded. "I understand."

I gaped at him. He did? She was telling him he would be kicked out, or killed, and he was okay with that?

But before I could protest, Darcy went on, "I haven't had time to discuss matters with the council yet, but know that all of you will be punished for this stupid act." She turned her glare to Ellie. "I know your punishment. You're forbidden to set foot inside this enclave again. After this meeting, someone will drive you back to Broken Hill, and I expect to never see you here again."

Ellie's face paled.

"But—"

"And you," Darcy cut me off. Whatever protest I was about to blurt out was lost in my throat. "I expected more of you, Mirella. After all, you are our heart maiden. You shouldn't make up lies about connections to Damara and fake heart flowers and put your life at risk like that. You know how important you are to our enclave. To all enclaves. You can't lie like this, especially not to us." Her eyes darkened. "You're punishment will be more severe. Be ready." She sighed. "I have to go back to the infirmary now. You're all dismissed." She rushed out of the room.

Oscar cleared his throat. "We'll call on you again when we

have decided on your punishments. Now go."

Without another word, Oscar followed his mother out of the meeting room, and the other elder council members rose and started leaving.

I frowned, wondering if Artan had told them everything. I had seen him on the phone on our way down, that was how they knew to wait for our van and take Ryane to the infirmary, and Sloan's body. But had he told them everything? About the two kinds of alchemists we encountered? About my hallucinations? If he hadn't yet, I was sure he would. Telling the council about my episodes worried me, but telling them about the red alchemists seemed important.

When I turned around, Artan was already gone. Rye embraced Cora, who cried silently in his chest. Ramon started forward, and Theron walked out with Ellie.

I ran after my best friend. "Ellie ..."

She flinched when I halted by her side.

Theron put an arm over her shoulder and pulled her closer to him. "What do you want?"

My brows curled down. What? Did they expect me to hurt them? What the hell? "I just want to know how you are feeling," I said, trying to ignore Theron's hateful gaze. "Does it still hurt?"

"I'm okay," Ellie said, her voice barely a whisper.

"How is—?"

Theron cut me off. "I need to take her home before Darcy decides to lock her in our prison instead." He tugged her forward. "*Nais tuke.*"

I gawked at him, his words prickling like a bee sting, as he walked Ellie out of the building.

It took me a moment to be able to swallow the pain his words had dug in my chest and move. When I left the building, the main square was almost deserted. Hopefully, everyone went back to bed since there was nothing anyone could do right now other than fret and cry.

As I dragged my feet across the square, I realized something

Maybe it was better this way.

Even if my friends weren't angry with me, even if they were just quiet and throwing glares my way because the entire situation sucked and we could all punch a wall and cry buckets, I was still a danger to them. I had proved that one too many times. I made rash decisions, lied thinking I was helping, but only ended up making matters worse, and trusted too easily.

This was all my fault. They were all suffering and hurting because of me. It wasn't safe for them to be around me anymore.

And I could use this quietness and temporary anger to distance myself from them.

To make them safe.

I was so lost in this new realization, I barely notice someone was standing outside my house, waiting for me.

Dolan. My father.

I almost tripped when I saw him, but I pushed past the shock and continued my walk home.

Since I was hurt my friends were giving me the cold shoulder, I decided to not do that to him. After all, he wasn't the one to blame here. He didn't know about me, and when he found out, he wanted to tell me. My mother was the one who stopped him.

I glanced at him as I reached for the front door. "Good night."

"Mirella, wait." My hand paused on the knob, but I didn't

turn to look at him. "Ramon just told me that he told you the truth." He let out a loud sigh. "I'm sorry I didn't tell you before. I wan—"

"I know." I turned and faced him. For the first time, I analyzed his face, his features. A long sharp nose, round eyes, high cheekbones. How hadn't I noticed before we shared some of the same features? "I know you wanted to tell me and my mother wouldn't allow you to. Don't worry, I'm sure she and I will argue about that soon enough."

"I ... don't be too mad at her," he said. "Try to understand her."

I pressed my lips together, not sure I could do that. "You're a good man."

He looked me from head to toe. "Are you okay? Were you hurt?" The worry in his eyes made my heart squeeze with longing.

"No, I'm fine. Just tired."

"Right. Of course." He took a large step back. "I'll let you rest, then. And talk to your mother after that. But later, I would like to talk to you."

I nodded, fighting against the tears threatening to spill at any moment. "We can do that."

"Go in." He waved me off.

Emotion filled my chest; I thought it would burst. But I was able to keep that, and the tears, in, and entered my house. Seated at the bottom of the staircase on the foyer, my mother was waiting for me.

Her eyes widened, and she jumped to her feet once she saw me.

Taking in a deep, calming breath, I closed the door and faced her.

"I'm so glad you're finally home." She wrapped her arms

around me. I didn't hug her back. "I was so worried." Noticing I was standing there like a wax figure, she pulled back. "What happened?"

"Let's see, alchemists attacked us on the way there, Ramon became a werewolf, booby traps almost killed me, we fought a dragon, and then alchemists killed Sloan, and Ryane is in a critical state."

She gasped. "By Saint Sara-la-Kali ..."

"But that's not all." I paused, waiting to deliver the blow. "Ramon also told me something very interesting." Her eyes widened. Rage coursed through me, and I wanted to scream at her. "Why did you let me believe my father was a *gadjo*? Why did you let me spend so much time in Bellville without telling me the truth? Why do you always lie and hide things from me?" My voice rose with each question. "Why?"

Her face went white and her lower lip trembled. "I ... I ..."

I saw it coming before she uttered any words. More lies. If she said anything, it would be only more lies. The rage faded from my veins and sadness replaced it. I was sad for us, for our relationship. When I thought we were finally getting along well and developing a great bond, I found out about more lies.

My chest sank. "You know what? Don't bother. I'm tired of asking for the truth, *all of the truth*, and being lied to every-time. I'm done." I stomped past her.

She spun with me, her eyes wide. "W-what are you going to do?"

I didn't look at her as I went up the stairs and said, "First thing tomorrow morning, I'm asking the council for my own house."

I heard her gasp, but I didn't feel anything. From this moment on, my heart was shielded from her.

25

Even though every muscle in my body hurt, I couldn't fall asleep. I tossed and turned in bed for hours until I gave up. Mumbling some nonsense about needing to rest, I shot up from bed and put on a heavy jacket over my pajamas, beanie, gloves, and boots with fleece interior.

I stepped out onto the porch and two warriors stepped out from the shadows—Leander and Lash. I sighed, wishing they stayed out of my sight so I could pretend I was alone and free.

Doing my best to ignore them, I stepped out onto the street, thankful most of the paths had been shoveled and now there were only little mounds of snow accumulated against the walls.

However, there was nothing to be done about the cold. I tightened my jacket, cursing myself for needing to get out of that stuffy house. It was all my mother's fault. If she hadn't been a terrible mother, if she hadn't lied to me so much and pushed me away, I would be fine with sinking into the couch and watching TV until I fell asleep.

But, as it was, I couldn't stay in there with her. I didn't want to hate her, but I couldn't control my feelings right now.

I stopped by the edge of the forest, where I usually liked to take my time and clear my mind, but the chilly wind was strong here. It bit my face, and I had to pull the collar of my jacket up to protect myself. I tried enduring it, but after three minutes, I gave up and resumed my slow walk around the enclave.

I was crossing the main square when Artan stepped out of the infirmary.

His amber eyes found mine, and the sadness and indifference in them made my heart sink.

He glanced around, as if considering to bolt. Thankfully, he latched on to his honor and didn't turn away when I approached him.

"How's Ryane?" I asked, my voice low.

"She's better." His voice was hard. Cold. "My *puri daj* has been healing her nonstop. She thinks Ryane is out of danger now." He paused, his jaw ticking. "But it'll take a while for her to recover fully."

I placed a hand over my aching heart. "That's ... a relief." If Ryane had succumbed to her injuries and blood loss, I wasn't sure I could endure it. There were too many dead and injured tziganes piling on my shoulders. I would soon cave and crumble under such heavy weight. "I'm sorry."

Artan frowned. His hands curled into fists. Tears burned the back of my eyes.

"I ..." He pressed his lips into a think line before continuing, "I know you're not responsible for all that happen. My mind is sure of that, but the pain in my chest says otherwise. I'll need some time." He retreated a foot. "Until then, I think it's better if I step down from your training. I'm sure Theron will be happy to train you."

Those words hurt more than he would ever know.

"I understand," I whispered.

Without another word, Artan nodded and marched away. My heart broke into tiny pieces as I watched him leave.

Leaving me.

For good.

I had been trying to push him away for weeks, but I think that deep down I hoped we would find a way to work it all out and be together in the end. Maybe Kizzy would fall in love with someone else. Maybe I would be able to convince the council of letting the heart maiden have a partner. I didn't know exactly how, but now as I watched him walking away, I knew I had hoped so much for a miracle to happen.

But now it was really over. After all that had happened in the past few days, I knew it was all over. At first, I had lost my trust in him, and just when I thought I could get it back, he lost his trust in me.

There was no coming back from that.

I sucked in a sharp breath and raised my head. It was better this way. Artan and I were not meant to be anyway. Even with all the hope in the world, I couldn't make miracles happen. Now, he was free to learn to love his fiancée, and I was free to be the best heart maiden I could.

Because so far, I had been a pretty bad one.

I sat at the edge of the fountain in the center of the main square. It was empty—the water had finally been drained since the weather turned cold. The bottom of the fountain was peppered with coins and other small tokens that had been thrown in with wishes.

If I threw a small token in it and made a wish, would it come true? Because I had so many wishes and none of them seemed possible.

I closed my eyes and remembered what I was: the heart maiden.

I might not have wanted to be the heart maiden, but I understood its importance now. Being the heart maiden was an honor. It was an important duty, if not the most important in the tzigane world. I was the only one who could find the heart flowers and save my kind. I tried feeling proud of it, of my calling. Most of the time, I did. Then, my friends got hurt because of my poor choices, and I regretted it immensely.

I inhaled deeply.

I couldn't dwell on what had already happened and change it. I just had to make sure I would be better from now on. I would be one hell of a heart maiden.

Or I would die trying.

I was about to stand and go back home when the dull pain started behind my eyes. It spread quickly, and I blinked fast as my sight darkened.

Suddenly, a burst of light exploded around me. I shielded my eyes with my hands from its brightness. Once it started fading, I lowered my arms and gasped.

"Hi, Mirella."

I gawked at Damara, seated at the edge of the fountain beside me. There was water in the fountain, flowers in the flowerbeds around the square, the sun shone high, and the snow was gone. I glanced around and didn't see one living soul, not even Leander and Lash, who were supposed to follow my every step.

"Is this another hallucination?"

"No," she said, her voice calm. "It's a vision."

"Go away, Damara." I closed my eyes. "I don't know if you're real or not, and I don't care. Just stop showing yourself to me."

"I'm here to prove I'm real. I mean, I can visit your mind during the visions."

I snapped my eyes open. "How?"

"I'm going to tell you the truth, then I'll let you know how to confirm it."

I narrowed my eyes at her. "Truth about what?"

"The truth behind your pain, your tremors, your visions, and your sleepless nights. The truth the elder council can't find out ... if you want to live."

"W-what?"

She offered me a sympathetic smile. "The heart maiden is a special and powerful tzigane. With every flower the heart maiden finds, the more powerful she gets. However, too much power makes for an unstable mind." Her smile turned wicked. "With so much power, the heart maiden goes crazy. Absolutely crazy. The symptoms you're presenting? The pain, the tremors, the visions, and the insomnia? They are the beginning of the craziness. With time, it'll only grow worse. You'll lose control, you won't know who is friend or foe, and the visions will assault you every few minutes. You won't know what's real and what's not."

"So ... what happens then?"

"When the heart maiden starts losing control, the elder council prepares an accident. The heart maiden dies before she can hurt anyone."

I gasped. "What do you mean by accident?"

"The elder council kills the heart maiden, and they cover

it up by making it look like the heart maiden was sick, or in battle ... take your pick."

I couldn't catch my breath. "That can't be. The tziganes depend on the heart maiden, the elder council works with the heart maiden ... how, why would they kill her?" Why would they kill *me*?

"Because they can't control her." She paused. "I only learned about all this after I faked my own death, but by the time I ran away, I was already more advanced than you are. And the elder council knew. They kept an eye on me even closer than before. It was hard to sneeze without a warrior being all over me. They were waiting. Once my condition deteriorated more, they would have taken me out."

I stood from the fountain's edge. "You're lying."

"After I learned about this, I investigated. All the heart maidens before me were killed and their records were moved into a secure place." She stood and faced. "I'll tell you where it is and how to get in and you'll see for yourself."

"W-why are you doing this?"

Once more, her smile sent a shiver down my spine. "Call it a heart maiden bond."

I shook my head. Heart maiden bond? What was she trying to pull off here? "I don't believe you."

"I said I can prove it to you." Then, she told me exactly where and how to find the records about the previous heart maidens. "Go there and you'll see for yourself."

Another burst of light flashed around me, and I closed my eyes against it. When I opened them again, Damara was gone. The square was back to normal: fountain without water, almost no flowers in the flowerbeds except for ever-greens, snow accumulated in the corners, and the two warriors standing a few feet from me, their gaze impassive as they scanned the square.

The pain still rang inside my head, but it felt like a bad headache, nothing I couldn't deal with.

Despite the pain, my mind whirled. What the hell had Damara told me? Could I believe her? What if it had been all in my mind, and every word she said was part of my imagination?

I can prove it to you.

If I followed her instructions, if I went where she told me to, would I find the records? I was eager to go check them, but I was also afraid. Because if I found them, if everything was there, then it meant Damara really was able to enter my mind, and it meant her words were right.

I had to check it for myself.

Determined, I marched into the library building, right beside the main building where the offices and the elder council was located. Leander and Lash followed me inside, but as usual, they kept their distance.

The library was bigger than I remembered—I had only come in here once before, when I had been with Darcy. At the time, I hadn't paid much attention to the place, but now that I walked through the long rows of shelves filled with books at night, my focus was sharp. I turned on the front lights of the library, but I stepped into the shadows as I advanced to the back. I could have turned on all the lights, but then the warriors would easily see what I was doing, and for some reason, I wanted to be quiet about this.

Like Damara had instructed me, I walked to the far back of the library, where there was a section where the bookshelves all turned to themselves, forming a perfect square lined with the wall—the same wall from the main building to the left.

I halted before the wall where it met the corner, half of the space hidden behind the side of a tall shelf. I put my hand on the space where Damara had instructed.

"Two feet from the wall, three feet from the floor," she had said.

I focused, channeling my power, and imagined an invisible lock clicking. A second later, a faint click sounded. My eyes widened, but I didn't stop. I imagined the wall moving into itself, like a sliding door. A second later, the wall moved, opening a passageway.

Stunned, I walked into the secret room.

I turned my palm up and conjured a flame. It illuminated the space, revealing a long, heavy wooden table in the middle, and many shelves around it. The shelves contained leather-bound books, scrolls, and loose papers.

Following Damara's directions, I walked around the table and halted before the shelf with red marking on its side. I ran my fingertips over the markings. I had no idea what they meant, but I was sure they weren't there just for decoration.

I checked the dates on the spine of the books on that shelf.

I grabbed the first one Damara mentioned. From 1500s to 1800s. I flipped it open and scanned through the pages. My heart squeezed tight as I confirmed all she had said.

Florence, the heart maiden before Damara. She had been twenty-five when she died by the hands of an alchemists during a mission to retrieve a heart flower.

Kezia, the heart maiden before Florence. She had been twenty-three when she died of pneumonia, followed by multiple organ failure.

Charity, the heart maiden before Kezia. She had been twenty-eight when she died from a spell the alchemists had cast upon her when trying to retrieve a heart flower.

Hester, the heart maiden before Charity. She had been twenty-one when she died during a fight against revenants. They had attacked her camp when she went after the heart flower.

The entries went on and on. All the heart maidens in this book—it went back for three hundred years before Damara—had died young, between twenty and thirty years old. As for the cause of death, I wasn't so sure. A heart maiden could die when attacked by revenants, or from a poison-like potion from the alchemists, or when fighting alchemists.

But it didn't stop there.

Damara had told me what to do next.

Calling my magic, I rested my hand on the cover of the book and invoked the truth. A faint orange light shone from the book's closed pages. When I opened the book again, the cause of death of all heart maidens was different from before—but they were all the same thing.

The *Yog Ozi Nas*—Fire Heart Fever.

I dropped the book as if it had burned me.

It couldn't be.

It just couldn't.

Because ... if this was true, then it meant I was going crazy. It meant the Fire Heart Fever was starting, and if the elder council found out about it, they would kill me.

Slightly less aggravating, it also meant Damara and I really had a connection, and she could enter my mind at will.

"Mirella?" Leander called.

I picked up the book and put it back on the shelf. Then, I

scurried out of the secret room—the wall slid back into place —and grabbed a random book from the nearest shelf.

"Here," I called out.

One second later, Leander stepped into the square formed by the wall shelves. "There you are. I heard a loud thud. Are you okay?"

"Yes, I'm fine." I waved the book I had in my hands. "I dropped the book. That must be the sound you heard."

"That must be it." He narrowed his eyes and glanced around. "I don't think I've ever been to this corner before." He fixed his eyes on the book in my hands. "The Hidden Meaning of Colors and Emotions. Hm."

Heat of embarrassment spread through my cheeks. "As heart maiden, I'm trying to learn everything I can."

"Of course." He stepped out, but I sensed his presence a couple of feet out of the square.

Letting out a long breath, I sank to the ground and hugged my knees. My body felt numb and heavy, and I couldn't breathe.

So ... it seemed I was going crazy and the elder council would kill me.

Death is coming for you.

The words of that Romani woman came back to haunt me. I thought it had been a mean joke, but I wasn't so sure now. Perhaps she had seen something. She had known about my future.

Regardless, I now had to come up with a plan: How to trick the elder council so they wouldn't find out I was going crazy and kill me.

I wouldn't feel this scared and lost if I had my mother and my friends to help me out, but I couldn't count on them anymore. My mother was a lying machine, and I was a danger to my friends.

My heart hurt as I thought about my bleak future: lost, alone, and about to die.

Continue reading about Mirella's adventures on *Soul Wanderer*, book 4 of The Fire Heart Chronicles!

THANK YOU

Thank you for reading *Sorrow Bringer*!

Reviews are very important for authors. If you liked my book, please consider leaving a review on your preferred online store and/or on goodreads, please!

You can get the next book on the series now:

Soul Wanderer

Don't forget to sign up for my Newsletter to find out about new releases, cover reveals, giveaways, and more!

If you want to see exclusive teasers, help me decide on covers, read excerpts, talk about books, etc, join my reader group on Facebook: Juliana's Club!

ABOUT THE AUTHOR

While USA Today Bestselling Author Juliana Haygert dreams of being Wonder Woman, Buffy, or a blood elf shadow priest, she settles for the less exciting—but equally gratifying—life as a wife, a mother, and an author. She resides in North Carolina and spends her days writing about kick-ass heroines and the heroes who drive them crazy.

Subscribe to her mailing list to receive emails of announcement, events, and other fun stuff related to her writing and her books: www.bit.ly/JuHNL

For more information:
www.julianahaygert.com

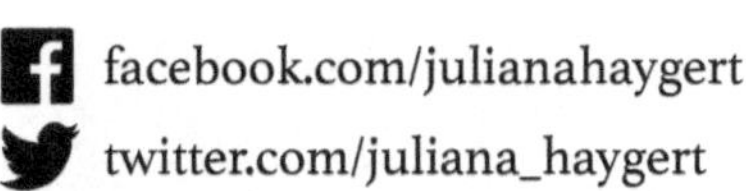

facebook.com/julianahaygert
twitter.com/juliana_haygert
instagram.com/juliana.haygert

ALSO BY JULIANA HAYGERT

www.julianahaygert.com/books/

Free

Into the Darkest Fire

Tested

Rite World: Blackthorn Hunters Academy

The Demon Kiss (Book 1)

The Hunter Secret (Book 2)

The Soul Bond (Book 3)

The Shadow Trials (Book 4)

The Infernal Curse (Book 5)

Rite World

The Vampire Heir (Book 1)

The Witch Queen (Book 2)

The Immortal Vow (Book 3)

The Warlock Lord (Book 4)

The Wolf Consort (Book 5)

The Crystal Rose (Book 6)

The Fire Heart Chronicles

Heart Seeker (Book 1)

Flame Caster (Book 2)

Sorrow Bringer (Book 3)

Earth Shaker (Novella)

Soul Wanderer (Book 4)

Fate Summoner (Book 5)

War Maiden (Book 6)

The Everlast Series

Destiny Gift (Book 1)

Soul Oath (Book 2)

Cup of Life (Book 3)

Everlasting Circle (Book 4)

Willow Harbor Series

Hunter's Revenge (Book 3)

Siren's Song (Book 5)